I0723330

BETWEEN HEAVEN & 42ND AND BROADWAY

BY

MICHAEL CAISSIE

Briley & Baxter Publications | Plymouth, Massachusetts

Paperback ISBN: 978-1-954819-76-4
eBook ISBN: 978-1-954819-66-5

Book Design: Amy Deyerle-Smith

*This book is dedicated to my late grandmother, Ann Crowley,
who always encouraged me to just keep writing.*

PROLOGUE

A SINGLE BEAD OF SWEAT trickled down exposed skin. It glistened in the moonlight that pooled into the small room through the single window. Lips and tongue persistently followed it, stopping periodically to kiss and nibble just enough to elicit soft moans from parted lips.

She arched her back, welcoming the touch of his big, strong hands, along with his lips and tongue that continued their way down her yearning body. Their two forms, intertwined as they became one, moved in a slow, sensual rhythm with each other, both quickly approaching their desired crescendo. Her sighs of pleasure increased in intensity as he turned her over, continuing to thrust as his aggression started to shift.

The nuzzling kisses across her vulnerable body became bites that were a little too intense, and her moans were replaced with gasps that lived somewhere between pleasure and pain. But she didn't put a stop to it, not even when he grabbed a good handful of hair and pulled it. The slow sensual rhythm, that gentle intimacy between them, was now gone, replaced with something far more animalistic.

Faster and faster they continued, the sounds between them that mere moments ago were the sounds of making love replaced with the sounds of unadulterated fucking. Their inevitable climaxes approached, but it would never actually come to fruition.

Somewhere in the distance, a shrieking baby crying in a nearby crib put an end to the carnal moment; a moment that, in reality, was never anything more than a fantasy. The crying baby was Paul's daughter, and the woman, who was still fast asleep next to him, was his wife. For years, long before she was ever his wife, she was always the object of his sexual desires, but now those desires were mere illusions.

The baby continued to cry, while his wife continued to sleep.

This was Paul's life now. This was a life that, on the surface, felt as fake and as empty as his sexual fantasy that had drifted away into the warm night air.

The bed was the same, and so were the two players, but outside of his imagination, there was nothing sexual between them now. She lay, as she always did nowadays, teetering on the edge of her side of the bed, with her back to him, wearing a simple and bland nightie. There was nothing sensual about it, outside of the slightest glimpse of her ass-cheeks peeking out of white panties. He lay on his back, shirtless and covered in sweat, not from anything sexual, but rather from the night's hot and sticky air that permeated their closet of an apartment. An old and tired box-fan rested in the window, but its efforts always seemed pointless to him, especially this time of year. It was mid-summer in New York. It was fucking humid.

He was wide awake.

So was the colicky baby.

His wife was not.

This was Paul Stephenson, twenty-seven years old, physically handsome in every way imaginable. There was something lost in his eyes, though, a heavy sadness trapped amongst his masculine beauty. He lay staring at the ceiling for a beat as the baby's crying continued, its mother still fast asleep.

"I'll get her," he finally hissed, climbing out of bed and trudging over to the nearby crib. He leaned in and picked up the still screaming baby. "Shh. It's okay. Daddy's got you."

The sound of his voice soothed the tiny bundle in his hands as he lay his child on the foot of the cramped bed before he changed the overdue dirty diaper. There was a genuine kindness in him throughout this exchange, a proud father openly glowing with his love for his young daughter.

"There you go," he said, putting the finishing touches on a fresh diaper. "You hungry? Guessing you're hungry?" Paul asked, as he dutifully carried his child toward his slumbering wife, gently nudging her with one arm as he continued to rock the baby.

"Hey. She's hungry," got him no answer though. Another gentle nudge, along with, "Baby, come on," finally got him something resembling a response.

Something started to shift behind his eyes, the warmth that was on display just a moment ago had dissipated, replaced with something far colder.

Despite the sudden shift, he still did his best to remain calm and cool on the surface as he spoke.

"You know I can't feed her, Valentina," was what finally managed to get the cute girl-next-door type that he called a wife to stir. She took out her breast, sheerly out of instinctual repetition at this point, and brought the baby to it. Paul watched for a moment, conflicted, before turning away and heading toward the door.

"I can't sleep," he muttered. "I'm nervous about tomorrow, and it's too fucking hot." He paused for a moment, expecting some kind of answer, but both mother and daughter were both too preoccupied to pay any mind to his concerns. He continued anyway. "I'm... I'm going to get some air. Maybe get some work done." He stared across the moonlit room at the woman he had once loved to the point of distraction. Now he was just hoping for some kind of response—but nothing was forthcoming. Paul turned away, with his already sad eyes somehow managing to look even sadder.

———

Paul splashed water on his face and stared at himself in the bathroom mirror. Scars from several bullet wounds decorated his upper back. The scars were prominent, tragically beautiful even, and there were enough of them to suggest Paul had seen his fair share of gun violence. But like the crudely done tattoos littered across various parts of his body, the bullet wounds were a distant memory to him; memories of moments that had been pushed way down inside his soul, hopefully forever.

Hopefully...

> *Conventional wisdom would say that nothing should ever be wound too tight. That there's only so much give to that reflection that stares back at you before the inevitable happens.*

Paul pulled on a t-shirt, before taking out the last Lucky Strikes cigarette from a crumpled pack and lighting it up. Marlboro, with their flip-top box, had been his smokes of choice for years, but that was before he served the greatest country in the world. He had switched over to the Lucky Strikes by chance, after the third or fourth time he received a four-pack of them included with his issued C-Rationed meal. Ten different brands were offered as a companion to the meals, but the more popular brands were always in short supply. Of course, soldiers who served after 1975 didn't have to wonder what brand they would get, as cigarettes were removed from the accessory packs altogether, due to health concerns. By that point, though, Paul was back to being a civilian.

The first few times Paul couldn't get his hands on his desired choice he was able to trade for them from a non-smoker, with the trade usually costing him a can of fruit from the MRI boxes. Eventually, though, he found himself missing the fruit, and decided switching brands was the better route to go.

As Paul pulled a particularly long drag off of the burning smoke, his eyes returned to the mirror, falling on the red end of the cigarette. His gaze followed the smoke upwards, as it trickled out from his mouth and nose until he was finally staring back into eyes still full of such sorrow. Perhaps those sorrowful eyes were just another visual reminder of a painful past he was desperately trying to forget or perhaps the pain was from more recent triggers, ones that had nothing to do with bullets and bloodshed but lay a lot closer to home.

But what happens before the break? What happens as the cracks start to grow, from tiny spiderwebs, to...something just short of full-blown chasms?

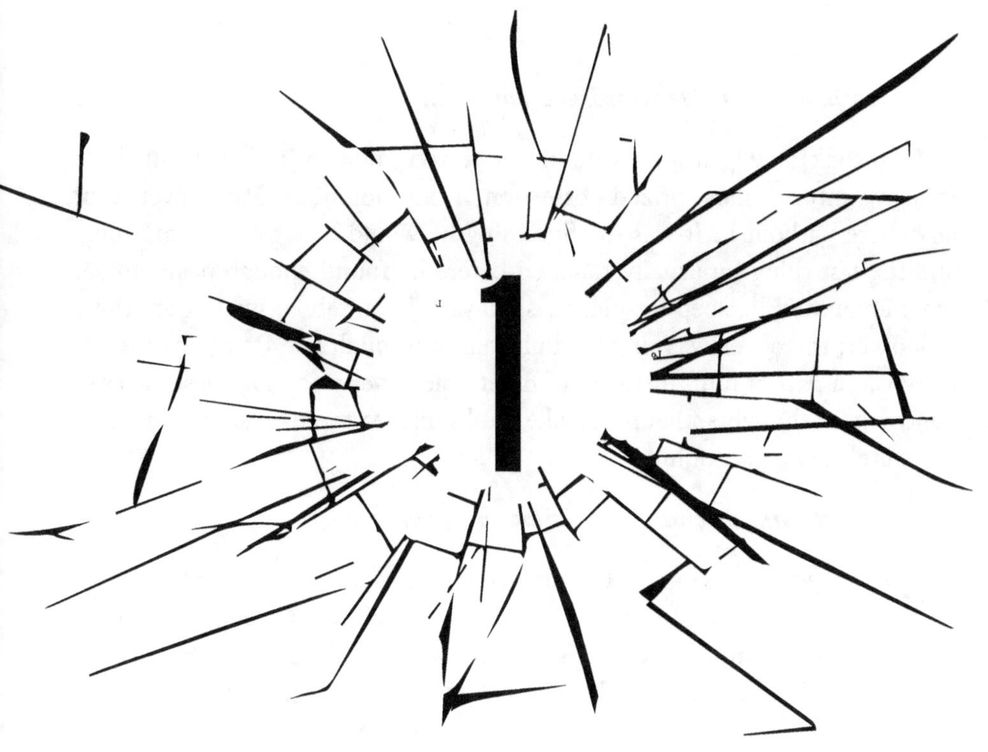

MANHATTAN: Sunday July 10th, 1977

A GRAFFITI-RIDDLED SUBWAY CAR, LITTERED with discarded trash, carried a small handful of late-night misfits through the New York night. Dressed in jeans, boots, and a bomber jacket, Paul looked as if he still belonged in the previous decade, as he sat amongst the scattered few.

His eyes scanned the endless words, most of it indistinguishable gibberish sprayed in an eclectic color pallet across the car, before his attention fell on one coherent piece written in red: *the Devil prowls around like a roaring lion, seeking someone to devour.*

Paul stared at the words. The paint from the letters had dripped before they had dried, giving them an ominous look, like they had been written in actual blood. *This was New York in the late '70s, so perhaps it had been written in blood*, Paul thought, as he continued to stare at the Biblical phrase in front of him. He read the words over and over again, before finally turning away, and allowing his mind to drift elsewhere, eventually arriving back to some thoughts of his own.

What happens when those chasms are as far and as wide as the human eye could ever see? Do we even have to actually crack and break before we become nothing more than foaming animals, jaws open, teeth bared to the world around us...

Paul took a swig from his flask, before returning to jotting down those thoughts into his most prized possession, a tiny notebook. Paul never went anywhere without it. It was the first thing he would look for each morning, and the last thing he usually touched before he found enough peace to get what amounted to sleep for him these days. The notebook wasn't anything to look at; the cover was simple, dull even, but much like Paul's exterior, it truly was a part of him. Inside that forgettable cover were countless pages of handwritten thoughts, that much like Paul's insides, were tattered and worn, but were truly a part of him.

...just dying to scratch some innate and primal itch?

He looked up, taking in the sorrowful state of affairs of those in the car with him, a state about to get a whole lot worse for one patron in particular. There weren't many of them, and the majority, much like the subway car they were riding in, had clearly seen better days. Their clothes and overall being were unkempt, their bloodstreams flowing with drugs, alcohol, or in some cases both. Most were subdued from their bad habits, or strictly from the late hour, but not all of them were ready to call it a night when it came to their chosen debauchery.

"Check out this motherfucker!" came out of the toothy-grin of one of four youthful hoodlums as they approached an old drunk who was slumped over on the seat across from Paul. They were a physically imposing bunch, once children of the street, now graduated to full-fledged and hardened gang members.

A product of their environments, each one had their own tragic story that could easily fill the pages of some heartbreaking book, but this wasn't their story; it was Paul's. Besides, it was painfully clear they had no intention of sharing any sad tales at the moment. They had other things on their minds, as one of the hoodlums looked straight at Paul, while the others took to going through the passed-out drunk's pockets.

Rolling a drunk while they were passed out was known as a lush-working, and for many at the time, it was considered an actual profession of sorts. Of course, Paul didn't know anything about this personally, but he had read about it in *Junky*, a book from one of his literary idols, William Burroughs.

Burroughs' original title of choice for his seminal book had simply been *Junk*, but the publishers baulked at the title, fearing the general public would believe the book was actual garbage. Instead, the publishers decided on the title of *Junkie: Confessions of an Unredeemed Drug Addict.*

The title wouldn't be the only thing the publishers would meddle with either, forcing Burroughs to remove some of the more controversial aspects of the book, particularly when it came to homosexuality. It wouldn't be until 2003, and the release of the 50th anniversary edition of the book, that Burroughs' original text would be shown to the public thanks to the eminent Burroughs scholar, Oliver Harris. Harris would title the definitive edition of Burroughs' seminal first novel *Junky*, and included the author's own unpublished introduction, along with those missing controversial aspects from the original publication.

The book was originally released in 1953. Burroughs was thirty-nine years old at the time. He thought the book was timely then, but it was even more so now with the booming heroin epidemic. Even more important than being timely or timeless, though, *Junky* was deeply personal for Burroughs, something Paul's editor had never accused any of his manuscripts of being. This drastic difference between the two was certainly not lost on Paul.

In *Junky*, Burroughs has said that being a junky was a way of life, because he himself was a junky. Paul wasn't a junky, far from it. He wasn't sure what he was at this point, and maybe that indecisiveness found its way into his manuscripts. Maybe that indecisiveness was just Paul's uninspired way of life.

Paul had three finished manuscripts, the last of which he was still waiting to hear back about, but the other two had already faded into the nothingness like the rest of Paul's life. Paul still had copies of both of them, collecting dust somewhere in their tiny apartment, which was a probably a better end for them than the copies he had given to his editor. Paul was certain those manuscripts had found their way into one of the uptown dumpsters long ago, the pages now littering about the endless piles of garbage at the Fresh Kills Landfill on Staten Island. The thought of his pages, soiled and rotting away, somewhere in the 2,200 acres of the world's largest landfill, seemed like some kind of cruel poetic justice to Paul, and at one time, he actually considered it a possible message from a higher power.

Paul had thought about quitting writing altogether after the second rejection, in the same way Burroughs had pretty much given up on writing before he wrote *Junky*. Paul had heard that if it weren't for Ginsburg imploring his good friend to continue, telling him that he *was* in fact a writer, *Junky* never would have seen the light of day.

Paul didn't have a Ginsburg in his life. He had an editor that hated his writing, and a wife that the only thing she hated more than Paul's writing, was being stuck married to Paul in the first place. But despite the glaring lack of support, Paul still hoped, and sometimes even prayed (although he didn't particularly care for prayer or even really believe in it), that the third one was the one. Unlike the previous two, this last one he knew was personal, and so he had high hopes this would be the one that would put him on the shelves, sitting side-by-side with his idols.

Then it would all have been worth it.

All of the bloodshed, the battle scars, the disappointments, heartaches, heartbreaks, doubt, and self-loathing, would then only be pages of the chapters in his life, instead of his whole life's story. Then he would finally be able to empty the discarded and pungent-smelling cigarette butts from life's ashtray for once, and at least partially cleanse himself from that lingering stench of depression that surrounded him.

Paul and the hoodlum held eye contact with one another until the thug had apparently seen enough.

"Fuck you lookin' at?" was spat in Paul's direction.

The man flashed a blade that really sold the desired answer to the rhetorical question, and it quickly brought Paul's eyes down to the pages of his notebook, just as the old drunk started to stir, and another tragic chapter in the hood's harrowing book was about to be written.

Unbeknownst to the hood, or anyone else in the train for that matter, that chapter would be one that directly affected his book's finale. But that was still a ways away from the current moment.

The old drunk blurted out, "What are you...?"

There was a moment of struggle before the cold steel of the blade met vulnerable flesh. The old man never finished his question, as he was stabbed, over, and over, and over, and over again. It was incredibly raw violence, the kind that led to the drunk's blood decorating the subway car, accenting the graffiti, along with anything—or anyone—close enough to fall victim to the trajectory.

Clearly in the line of fire, some of the blood spray splashed across Paul's boot. He noticed but tried to refocus on the pages in his hands. He was failing miserably, though, with his eyes continuously wandering back to the blood spatter on his boot. Like an obsession, or someone suffering from a case of OCD, Paul couldn't take his eyes off of his soiled footwear. Perhaps it was his equally soiled past, or perhaps it was just nothing more than his buried humanity, but regardless of the reason, the presence of the blood was crippling for him.

The old man lay covered in his own blood, gasping for air. Adding insult to injury, the hoods took turns spitting on him, before moving away as if nothing had happened just as the train started to slow for a stop. No one on the train had done a thing to help, including Paul. They had all stood by, either frozen in fear or total indifference, as the act of violence had unfolded before them. Paul was sure that on some level, most of them were just happy for it to be happening to someone else, and for it to be over.

Paul took one last look at the man—most likely dying from the knife wounds—along with the group that caused all the agony, before getting off at the stop. He didn't know it yet, but the moment wasn't over for him. In fact, it was just the beginning of something...something big ... something that would be just a small part of his bigger picture.

Paul found himself standing in the middle of what is colloquially known as *The Deuce*. All around him, lit storefronts housed the latest grind-house pictures, peep shows, and sex shops. Those looking for a cheap thrill could just as easily have found themselves mugged or even killed here before ever getting that desired taste of the underbelly of society.

The area was a backdrop for an eclectic group of pimps, junkies, prostitutes, and thrill-seekers. It was ultimately a concrete playground for the deprived and perverse, where the basic rules of humanity had fallen through the cracks in the sidewalk a long time ago.

Only adding fuel to an already raging fire was the fact that the heroin epidemic had just started to take a stranglehold on the city. The tiny microcosm of the population in front of Paul was certainly a reflection of the times.

> *Most of the junkies I know will tell you that their addiction was one of a gradual incline. That very few start with a needle in their arm.*

One of the numerous junkies scattered throughout the spot started to have a seizure on the sidewalk. No one seemed to notice or care, most actually stepped over him to continue on their way. Like loyal army ants, they instinctively walked over the fallen, moving through the soiled and puddle-riddled concrete, continuing on, one foot in front of the other, just doing whatever it took to get to see another day.

Paul stopped and stared at the junkie in obvious distress for a few seconds, before he got back in line like a good soldier. He continued onward, passing two beat cops who were busy harassing a young black pimp and his stable of girls. He finally stopped in between two neon signs: "Twenty-Five Cents Peep Shows, Books & Magazines," was written on one, and "Twenty-Five Cents Live Nude Girls, 8mm Films Novelties" on the other. The place was one of countless smut spots that populated the neighborhood. The area held no real significance to Paul, though, at least not yet, outside of the convenience of it being right in front of him.

> *That it takes time, perseverance, and patience, to build oneself into a full-blown addict. So who am I to think...*

Paul took out his trusty notebook, and once again started to write, before finishing the last of his thoughts for that particular moment, and heading inside the storefront.

...that I should be any different?

Once inside, Paul waded through the aisles, his attention only vaguely on what lined the shelves, and more on the people who populated the area. His voyeurism, part sincere intrigue, part sexually fueled, didn't go unnoticed by everyone in the place, however. The teller, a brick-house of a young woman, stared unapologetically at Paul, following his every move, and only taking her eyes off of him long enough to ash her Baby Virginia Slims cigarette.

With the majority of the shop's visitors being solo males, Paul's attention gravitated toward an interracial couple toward the back. He was a white middle-aged man, with gray hairs frosting the tips of his shaggy brown mane, and he wore an expensive suit that made him stick out like a sore thumb.

"You like that one?" the middle-aged man asked.

She was a beautiful African American youth, less than half his age, but despite their differences the two had obvious chemistry between them and could barely keep their hands off of one another.

"I donna know," she replied wide-eyed, with an innocent smile, as she nervously tugged at the ends of her shirt, her eyes never wavering from what he was holding in his hand. She was a youthful gazelle, with no shot of running to safety at this point.

"You don't? What do you know, sunshine?" he replied, biting his lower lip, his eyes never wavering from her soft and nubile body. He was the circling lion who had tackled his prey, his wanting jaws just hovering above her neck, preparing for the kill.

Paul watched as the man ran the fingertips of his right hand down the back of her jeans, as they continued to peruse the novelties on the shelves in front of them.

"You just choose something, baby. You know I'm not picky," she said, as he took to kissing her neck, his right hand still working its way down the back of those jeans. She eventually closed her eyes, just before a soft moan escaped from her youthful lips. *Maybe she was not some innocent lamb being led to slaughter after all*, Paul thought to himself, as he continued to study the couple.

The man's left hand had a wedding band. The ring finger on her left hand was barren. They were just two lustful people, who wanted nothing more than to fuck each other's brains out, regardless of the specifics, or of the consequences.

"Yo! What is it, babydoll?" came out like a roar from the owner of the spot, as he strutted in from the back of the store.

Byron was a nauseatingly thin man in his late forties, who was sporting some dark shades, and rocking a massive Afro. He came up behind the teller, placed his hands around her waist, and kissed her on the cheek.

The teller pointed toward Paul as she replied, "This cat's been in here more times than I can count the last few months."

The owner was all smiles, pulling her in closer despite the fact that she seemed indifferent to his advances. He was gross, slimy even, which was made even worse by the fact that she was more than breathtaking, and seemed completely out of place working in this joint.

"Repeat business is where it's at," Byron said but his good mood was going to be short-lived, as she just continued staring at Paul while Byron continued to rub up against her body.

"Yeah but he never buys anything, Byron. Just looks around, writing stuff in a notebook."

"Never buys...? Then why the hell didn't you kick his ass out?"

The teller smiled, biting her lip, as she continued to eye Paul. "I don't know. Probably. cause I think he's kinda foxy," she said, bringing Byron's fury to new heights.

"Oh hell no!"

With his face soured, Byron quickly made a beeline to Paul. "Say, Jack!"

Paul was too preoccupied with the couple to even see him coming.

"Hey! Talkin' to you, fuzz!" He was right in Paul's face now.

"Hey chill, man. I'm not a cop. I'm...I'm a writer."

He held up his notebook as his defense, but Byron looked less than convinced. He didn't let up. He had completely invaded Paul's personal space, causing Paul to try to back away; there wasn't whole lot of room to move, and he soon found his back against one of the bookshelves. He was stuck, and just like the teller, he was at the mercy of Byron's unwanted physicality.

"Man, quit talkin' all that static," Byron replied, as he ripped the notebook from his hand, and much to Paul's horror, took to looking at the pages inside.

"Hey, give it back! That's private, man!" was all Paul could muster, as he tried to physically take the book. But he stopped trying when the owner of the place balled up his fist, cocking it back as if ready to strike.

"Okay, man. Just...just chill," Paul added quickly, holding his hands up in defense.

With Paul effectively neutered, Byron went back to the notebook, flipping through more pages, while Paul reluctantly looked on. After page after page of internal turmoil for Paul, Byron finally spat out, "Shiiiiit," as he returned the notebook to him with a chuckle. "Not a pig alright...just a square. Look here, here's the skinny, you see? This ain't no public fuckin' library, so you either buy something or you get your ass outta here. You feel me?"

Byron leaned in real close to Paul, close enough to menacingly invade his space even more than he had already was. He lifted up the front of his shirt to reveal a handgun tucked into his waist, for some unnecessary, but very pointed emphasis.

"Okay. It's cool."

"It's cool?"

"Yeah, man."

Paul continued to eye the gun in Byron's waistband. It was a WW2-era Smith and Wesson Victory .38 revolver. Paul had been issued one himself when he was over in Nam. The double action .38 revolvers were issued to aircrews, because they were easy to use one-handed. Paul found his mind wandering, wondering if maybe this guy had served too. However, now wasn't really the time to find out.

Now was the time to make nice.

Satisfied with Paul's waved white-flag, the owner of the joint lowered his shirt and patted Paul on the shoulder before walking back to the counter and his teller almost as if nothing ever happened.

Paul looked at a neon sign above a doorway that was shielded by a drape advertising the Twenty-Five cent peep shows. He fished around in his pockets, eventually pulling out some change: a quarter, dime, and three pennies. He hesitated for a beat, contemplating his next move, and as he looked up he could see both the teller and the owner had their eyes glued on him.

"So who am I to think I should be any different?" Paul quietly asked himself.

He took one last look toward the couple, who were now literally trying to fuck each other standing up in the store, before ducking into the next room, notebook in hand.

———

Paul dropped a quarter into the slot, and nervously sat back to wait, stepping in something sticky in the process. He looked down at his boots, as he lifted them over and over again. The sound painfully signified there was clearly old residue spewed on the floor.

"Shit" escaped his lips, visibly somewhere between annoyed and disgusted, as he put his boots back on the ground, only to again notice the drying blood spatter from the subway car incident.

Paul started to squirm. Physically it was subtle, but it was coming from somewhere deep inside. It was that feeling you get when you're about to do something bad, and you're not sure if you're more excited or more scared of the possible consequences. Slowly the dark window in front of him started to come up. Inch by inch the barricade gave way to a sheet of plexiglass that had been clear at one time, but now was dulled with various scratches and graffiti. It was the last few moments, as the roller coaster cart struggled to pull itself to the approaching drop-off, its occupants a mixture of excitement and nerves, some even regretting being on the ride, but it was far too late to turn back now. Then the rollercoaster reached the top, and hesitated, nerves and anticipation at an all-time high before it finally went into...the free-fall.

Legs. Long, seductive, legs were the first bit of flesh that appeared before his eyes. They were eventually followed by the rest of a scantily clad seductress on the other side of the glass. She danced to the music, numb to everything at first, and not even looking at him, but when she finally did, she started to speak, but he couldn't hear her through the partition. Paul tapped his ears.

"What" I...I can't hear you!" he said, prompting her to mouth the words again, and although he still couldn't hear her, it was obvious now to him what she was saying.

"I'm...I'm cute? Thank...thank you," he said, blushing. For an attractive man, you'd think it was as if he was being complimented on his good looks for the first time. "You're really pretty!" he replied, causing her to tap her own ears. "I said you're really pretty!"

She smiled, running her hands along her body, as she stared at his crotch, prompting him to look down to his pants as well.

"Fuck. This is stupid," escaped from his lips. He felt embarrassed, flustered, anything but turned on, and looked towards the door to exit. But then she took off her top, revealing two perfectly perky breasts underneath. She had his full attention again, as she proceeded to rub her exposed breasts with her hands while continuing to dance, until the dark divider started to come down between them.

"Shit! What's happening?" he cried out, causing her to mimic putting more money into the slot, as the divider got lower and lower. "Fuck!" Paul looked at the loose change in his hands, none of it amounting to the needed quarter to see more, as a growing rage started to boil over inside him. This was going to be ugly.

Lower, and lower the divider went, until the dancer was completely out of sight, and Paul was left alone to stew in his anger. He started to pace around for a beat, before the sticky noises from his boots getting stuck to the floor caused him to start slamming his fists on the black divider repeatedly, with absolute and total reckless abandonment for his own well-being. Seeing blinding red now, he continued to unload on the divider with everything he had, until he had completely exhausted himself and managed to wound both of his big paws.

A boozy trail of smoke trickled off the end of a cigarette that rested in an ashtray on the bar. Paul watched the flame canoe the end of the cigarette, while he sipped the last of a well whisky on the rocks from his glass.

"Can I get another one, Vicky?"

The bartender, Vicky, was once a true beauty, but was now in her seventies. That, coupled with the harsh winters and the wear and tear that comes with working at a bar, meant she had obviously seen better days. You'd never know it, though, by the way she talked and carried herself.

She started to pour the refill, but stopped before a single drop hit the glass, causing Paul to look like he was about to cry.

"What?" he asked, incredulously.

She still didn't pour, and she didn't answer right away either. Paul just glared at the bottle, almost as if he was trying to will the booze into the glass with his painful desperation.

"I don't know how much longer I'm going to live, Paul," she replied finally, ending Paul's glare. He abruptly sat up straight, not exactly sure how to respond to her jarring declaration. His mind raced while he struggled to find the words, all while physically unable to look her in the eyes. This was more than hard for him. This was more than heartbreaking.

"Shit...hell of a way to tell someone that. What is it? Cancer?" he replied with the utmost sincerity in his voice, as he also managed to finally look up to make eye contact.

"It's whatever will get you to pay your tab, before I finally go," she said with a straight face.

He shook his head in disbelief, as all of the worry and heartache immediately washed away from those sincere eyes.

"Way to kick me while I'm down, you ole hag," Paul said, as he once again turned all of his focus and energy toward the glass that tragically still remained empty in front of him.

"Hey if the shoe fits, wear it, ya miserable prick."

Obviously pleased with herself, she smiled a grin riddled with missing teeth, before finally pouring him another drink. "Besides, looks like you're trying to beat me to the finish line?"

On his perplexed look, she motioned to his hands that had been poorly-bandaged with gauze now, so poorly so, that blood had already managed to soak through.

"Isn't this where you tell me I should see the other guy?" she asked, flashing yet another toothless grin.

"Why are you always so nice to me?" Paul asked meekly as he took a sip of his refill.

"Oh, I don't know…" She paused to think about it for a moment before, "Guess I just feel sorry for you is all."

"Gee thanks, Vicky."

Now there was no more sipping for Paul. He pounded the drink, and she quickly poured him another. This was a religious routine for them, that consisted of pour, drink, rinse, and repeat. It was a dance they had danced together countless times before, and it showed, as that dance continued now. It was effortless, like second nature, for both of them. It was a dance that took the two and made them into one.

"Or maybe I'm just trying to fuck ya."

She walked away with a cackle, leaving him with one of the few smiles anyone would ever see from him.

"Lucky me," he muttered under his breath.

"So, how's that book coming along?"

Paul went to pound his drink, but stopped, choosing instead to take out his notebook, while looking around the place, before finally answering. "Comes and goes," he replied, as he stared at a blank page in the notebook. But blank wasn't exactly the right word here, because where it certainly was void of any words, it was far from spotless, as a finger-sized bloody smear covered a quarter of the page. Was the smear the answer to what Vicky had said, Paul wondered. Were the pages of his notebook "the other guy" in the "you should see the other guy" scenario?

"Ha. Comes and goes…sounds like both of my ex-husbands," she replied. She was talking while doing side work, but made a point to look up at him every so often. She watched as his head was now in his pages. But he was still unable to write much of anything, which caused him to get noticeably uneasy.

It was late. It was really late, in the city that never sleeps, somewhere between night and the early morning, and the hour brought with it limited people in the bar. The scarcity brought a hazy silence. The kind of silence that feels like you might be dreaming. The unnerving quiet made Paul even more uncomfortable, as his eyes left the blood-smeared page to look out across the length of the bar.

"Can I get some change for the jukebox?" he asked, disgusted with both the blood-smeared page in front of him, and that dream-like feeling all around him.

"Oh, are we boring you already, Hemingway?" she replied without looking up from wiping down the other end of the bar.

"Never. Just thought some music would go nice with the stale ambience you have going on in here."

His words brought another genuine smile across Vicky's lips. Paul warmed her heart in ways she wondered if he would ever really be able to know. Just having him near made life better, and for that she was forever grateful, and because of that, she was often smiling when he was around.

"Well, it's preloaded. Just for you, babydoll. Just play something for me to dance to."

Paul downed his drink and lit up a cigarette before he made his way over to the jukebox, talking to himself along the way. "Something to dance to…" he said as he browsed his options, before finally settling on a selection.

Needless to say, his selection didn't exactly thrill Vicky, or any of the other patrons for that matter. A collective groan came from the peanut gallery as the moody, piano driven song played.

"For fuck's sake, Paul!" she cried out, throwing the dirty dish towel into a bucket to accent her obvious frustration. So much for all that gratitude for Paul warming her heart.

"Oh come on…dance with me," he said, even though the song was essentially a tragic plea for empathy toward human suffering, and didn't exactly elicit the mood for dancing. She tried to resist, to dismiss him even with a frustrated wave of her hands, but they both knew how this was going to end. She eventually relented, just like she had countless times before.

"Just make sure you keep your hands to yourself, because I'm a respectable and virtuous woman," she said, as she reluctantly joined him in the middle of the room.

"There isn't enough booze in this bar, or in the entire state of New York," Paul replied as they started to slow dance together. All jokes aside, and despite their obvious age difference, by this point it was more than obvious to anyone who cared to notice that they enjoyed each other's company. They were two lost souls, lost in a city of nearly sixteen million people, that had managed to find each other, and in doing so, had managed to actually soothe one another.

"You know…you're such a tease," she said, as she laid her head on his shoulder and they continued to dance.

MANHATTAN: Monday July 11th, 1977

PAUL SAT ALONE AT A table in the heavily populated Bickford's Coffee Shop on 42nd Street. Once a popular hangout for literary giants Jack Kerouac, William S. Burroughs, and Alan Ginsberg, the location, much like the rest of New York, had fallen victim to the times. In five short years the entire restaurant chain's foothold in New York would be nothing but a memory, but for now it still offered breakfast anytime, which worked well for an insomniac like Paul.

He would spend countless late nights or early mornings at the same table, writing in his notebook, hoping to channel just some of the magic from the writers who wrote here before him. Paul would often drift off, trying to imagine what it must have felt like to write the lines of Ginsberg's Howl, or what table Burroughs was sitting at when he was writing about being in Bickford's in Junky. These thoughts always started out as curiosity, inspirational at times, but they always ended on a sour note. A part of Paul always ended up thinking he had missed his chance to be one of those literary giants by being born in the wrong era. After all, the last great American novel was published in the 1950's.

What an awful realization for a struggling writer to have, Paul thought.

Tonight, just like countless other nights, Paul watched the comings and goings happening all around the bleak spot, with a fresh cup of coffee in front him. It was always an odd group of people, made up of two very different fronts. On the one hand there were all the misfits and freaks left over from a night out partying, and on the other you had the early birds, mostly blue-collar workers and civil servants.

Paul didn't exactly fit in entirely to either crowd, and he did little to displace being the odd-man-out, by constantly eyeing the others while writing in his notebook. He eventually looked up to a clock on the wall, staring at it for an extended period of time.

"You have time for another refill, Paul?" the waitress asked. She refilled his coffee before he even answered. She was cute as a button and all smiles, but she was also probably too young to even be working. Neither of these two things were lost on Paul, as he looked up at the two beautiful eyes that stared back at him.

"You kidding? I have time for several unfortunately," he replied, his eyes still lost in hers.

"Ever hear of sleeping to pass the time?" she asked with another inspired smile, as he finally broke their flirtatious eye contact to light up a cigarette.

"You know I could ask you the same thing, Linda."

"Yeah well, one of us is on the clock, and the other one is just watching it," she said, before walking away, going from table to table refilling coffees, and filling the time with more small talk.

"You got me there," he muttered as he sipped his coffee, watching her move about the place with unfiltered lust in his eyes. After a few poured refills for other guests, she eventually turned back with that same look. Oh shit.

Paul quickly looked away, his eyes moving back up at the clock on the wall, watching the second hand slowly tick, almost as if it were a grind for each second to pass. It was a little past four-thirty a.m., leaving Paul painfully caught between the approaching morning, and fleeing night. He watched that second hand continue to do its thing, as he drank his coffee, before lighting up another cigarette.

Later that morning, the second hand ticked around the face of a different clock now, this one on the wall of a stuffy office space, not much larger than a janitor's closet. It was now quarter past nine in the morning, as Paul sat in a folding chair on the other side of a desk, surrounded by stacks and stacks of books, manuscripts, and old magazines.

"Sorry to keep you waiting, Paul," Mr. Mackey said, taking Paul's attention away from the hands of that ticking clock. The packrat, and owner of the modest space, Mr. Mackey, was an overweight man in his sixties who was dressed like a million bucks. Paul never gave much thought to just how much Mr. Mackey's expensive attire was clearly at odds with the space he occupied, but unbeknownst to him, today was the day he was about to find out the reason.

"No, it's okay," Paul replied, as he stood up, all nerves, and extended his hand for the two to shake. Mr. Mackey either didn't see it, or he didn't care, choosing instead to plop himself in the seat behind the desk in a hurry.

"Have a seat," he replied.

Paul did, wiping the sweat from the palms of his hands on the front of his pants. Mr. Mackey was sweating too—several beads trickled down his forehead—but he did nothing about it, instead he just let it move down his face, until it eventually settled somewhere in the rolls of his neck, or on the collar of his expensive shirt.

"So, what'd you think?" The question lingered in the air unanswered by Mr. Mackey, who didn't even look at Paul, because he was too busy looking around his cluttered desk instead. The place was an epic sized disaster, with things thrown about, seemingly with no rhyme or reason to their placement. Paul found himself wondering how Mr. Mackey could find anything in the place, or how he could allow his place of business to look like this considering the numerous success stories he had had as an editor and publisher. Paul was well versed in those success stories.

At one point, Mr. Mackey had published three of the top ten best-selling books in the country, and that wasn't just a fluke, because it was the second time he had managed to have numerous titles on the list over the past decade plus. *Clearly, Mr. Mackey was great at his job*, Paul thought to himself, *but would it have killed him to hire an assistant to sort through this mess, and to keep his affairs more organized?* Again, unbeknownst to Paul at the moment, he would find out exactly why Mr. Mackey liked to work alone real soon.

"It's here somewhere," Mr. Mackey muttered under his breath, as he continued searching through the wreck, while Paul looked on like an impatient kid waiting to open presents on Christmas morning. At the moment, Paul didn't care about Mr. Mackey's attire, or why he was so messy, or why he didn't hire an assistant to help, because at the moment all he cared about was Mr. Mackey's opinion on his latest manuscript. All he cared about was what the man had to say about manuscript number three, the manuscript that was personal to him, the one that was unlike the previous two, the one that Paul was so sure would be the one to do it.

"Come on, you're killing me over here," Paul finally blurted out, unable to contain himself any longer, just as Mr. Mackey found the manuscript he was looking for, and finally looked up at Paul with it in his hands. "Just give it to me straight is all I'm asking, Mr. Mackey."

"Jesus, when was the last time you slept, kid?" he asked, staring wide-eyed at Paul, whose looks clearly warranted the question.

"I...I don't know. You know how I get. Come on. Is...is it any good?" Paul asked, his eyes pleading for some good news. Mr. Mackey just looked at him for a moment, genuine concern in his eyes, before sighing and putting on eye glasses.

"They left us face down in the mud?" He read the title of the manuscript, before taking off his reading glasses, and looking back up at Paul. "I don't know what to tell you, kid. I got about twenty pages in, and I can't sell this. It's too...it's scattered."

His words crushed Paul, both literally and figuratively, as he felt his insides twist and contort to the point of almost causing him to dry heave right there on this man's messy desk. How could this be happening to him? How could this be happening to him *again*? How many times did he have to hear rejection from a man who clearly knew his stuff, before it was time to start seriously considering burying his dream, or at least to consider walking out into traffic to help expedite the process of burying himself.

"But I'm too scattered." Paul stood up to plead his case. "My whole generation is fucking..."—Mr. Mackey's face cringed at the word choice—"Sorry...we're all scattered. Look around you, man." Paul's inner turmoil had a stranglehold on him now, as he sunk back down into the chair. "Please. I got a new baby. I...I need the money. I'm desperate." His last statement was spoken so low it was barely audible.

Mr. Mackey picked up the manuscript again, looking at it, and then back toward Paul and what was left of his shattered ego. "What do you want me to do, Paul? This isn't a fucking charity," he said, apparently a fan of swearing when the words were coming out of his own mouth, "Maybe...maybe it's time for you to hang up the idea of being a writer for a while."

Paul looked up, his eyes filled with glowing rage.

"Hey now, take it easy, kid."

Paul shook his head adamantly "no" over and over again before finally speaking. "This next one is going to be the one," he said, waving that well-worn notebook he was always carrying around, with a swell of momentary bravado escaping from him as the rage in his eyes was quickly replaced with a forced smile on his lips.

"I've been hearing about the next one for years from you. Speaking over here not as an editor now, but as a friend."

His words did little to settle Paul, though. He felt his mouth start to salivate, the spittle forming in both cheeks, as the nausea started to rise up, a part of the endless waves of inner torment that coursed through his very being. This was a nightmare.

Paul sat in that folding chair, heavy gunfire all around him, staring down at his stomach that was cut from end to end, forcing him to hold all seven and a half pounds of his intestines in his hands, while he cried out for a medic that would never come. No, this was worse than any nightmare. No, this was his hell.

"Then be a friend, Mr. Mackey. Help me out." That plastic smile was gone now, and the bravado, along with any ounce of pride he had left.

Mr. Mackey looked at Paul with sympathetic eyes for what seemed like an eternity.

"Look, you're up all hours of the night, for days on end, a friend would tell you to go home and get some sleep," Mr. Mackey finally said, as he stood up from his chair, those beads of sweat still pouring down his forehead, staining that expensive shirt-collar.

"Then be better than a friend then, because I don't need to hear that right now."

Paul's intense and unwavering eyes were glued on Mr. Mackey, as the man pushed some of the stacks of books out of the way, this time not struggling to find anything though. He knew clearly what he was looking for, and he knew exactly where it was, and after those books were moved, Paul saw the decent-sized wall safe that was hidden behind them.

"I'm not going to be your friend. This is business, and this here's what I'm willing to do for you. Hand me that leather bag over there."

Paul followed the pointed finger, before doing what he was told, then retrieved a brown leather satchel amongst the clutter, and handed it to Mr. Mackey.

Paul left Mr. Mackey's office shortly afterwards, the newly placed contents of that brown leather satchel providing the answers to why Mr. Mackey's expensive clothes didn't line up with shithole of an office space, and to why Mr. Mackey liked to work alone all these years. Paul didn't know it as he left the office carrying the satchel over his shoulder, but its contents would also provide Paul with answers to questions he didn't even know he had about himself.

It was early evening by then, as Paul made his way into his tiny New York apartment, his arms were filled with bags of groceries, diapers, and that wondrous brown leather satchel.

"Hey babe, I'm home!" he called out proudly, as he struggled to get the load inside, barely managing to do so, before practically dropping everything on the floor. "Babe?!" Despite the struggle, this was a new side to Paul. He was reinvigorated, lighter even.

He reached into one of the bags, taking out a sixer of Rheingolds. The New York Times once wrote, *Rheingold Beer was once a top New York brew*

*guzzled regularly by a loyal cadre of workingmen who would just as soon have
eaten nails as drink another beer maker's suds.*

At one-time it was the official beer of the New York Mets, but now Paul
was just happy he was even able to find the sixer, because the brewery had
closed up operations in 1976 when they were no longer able to compete with
the national chain-breweries.

Fucking corporations are slowly strangling the little guys, Paul thought, disgusted with the reality of the changing world all around him, as he opened
one of the beers, and quickly downed it. He was desperately trying to wash
the taste of that disgusting realization out of his mouth and out of his mind. So
much for being reinvigorated and lighter.

He finished the beer, wiping his mouth, and looked around the small apartment. It was deafeningly quiet, which only added to that lingering disgust still
in his mind. No wife. No baby crying. Just four walls of nothing but lonely
silence, a lonely silence that was plastered with tacky wallpaper, and a color
palette of the seventies consumed with oranges, greens, and browns.

Paul pulled a note that was stuck to the refrigerator door:

Went to visit my parents for a bit.

He stared at the note incredulously for a moment, before putting it back
where he found it and making his way over to a chair that sat in front of a
radio receiver.

Paul sat in the plaid-upholstery covered chair, the remaining beers and
the leather satchel in tow, before turning his attention to his three-year-old,
seventy watt per channel Marantz 2270 radio receiver. He ran his hand over
the smooth, wood-crafted cabinet that housed it before his finger fluttered
over the power button. He turned it on, the surging power bringing with it
the beautifully blue-tinted backlight that illuminated the tuning panel. Paul
ran his finger over the tuning knob, sliding it to the right, and methodically
moving through the mix of static and music, before eventually finding the
Mets game broadcast, with Lindsey Nelson and Bob Murphy doing the
play-by-play.

As Paul lit up a cigarette and cracked open another beer the congenial
tones of Lindsey Nelson cut through the lonely silence.

"George Mitterwald steps up to the plate in the top of the seventh, with
his Chicago Cubs trailing the home team Met's, but the Cubs' backstop has a
chance to change that with one on and two out."

"So far, though, he's 0 for two so far today, as he looks at ball one on
a pitch low and away from Jon Matlack, who has been pitching a gem today," Bob Murphy added on the telecast, just as Paul opened the satchel, and
peered inside.

"Mattlack goes into the windup, and delivers..." Murphy continued, as Paul closed the satchel, and leaned back into the chair,

"...and look out, Mitterwalk really got a hold of that one, sending the ball deep toward the centerfield wall, and...it's outta here. And just like that, we've got ourselves a tie ball game at Shea Stadium."

"You really hate to see that," Murphy added, "One mistake from an otherwise great outing, this late in the ball game, from Mattlack, who has struggled for most of the year, coming into the game with a three and eleven record."

Slowly their voices started to fade, as Paul finally started to drift off for some much-needed sleep, still sitting in that chair. The Mets would go on to win the game four to two, when their starting center fielder, Steven Henderson, hit a two-run homer off Bruce Sutter in the eighth inning, but Paul was already lost in his dreams by that point. The sounds of the broadcast were replaced by the sounds of AK-47's and RPG-2's being fired, seemingly from every direction, by Viet Cong forces.

He dreamt vivid dreams, the kind that felt so real he found himself wondering if he was in fact actually awake, that this wasn't just a dream, but a rehashing of real-life nightmare. Paul was back in Vietnam, back when he was a machine, back when he was programmed to kill without question, and back when he never actually feared death himself. There just wasn't time to fear it, so he, just like the other young men who were forced into service, just accepted death was just something that happened. To some it happened to them, but for others, like Paul, it happened all around them. At least that's how it happened in the real world. This was a dream, though, a nightmare really, and it didn't look as if Paul was going to make it home from this tour.

A human's large intestine weighs about four pounds, and their small intestine weighs around three and half pounds. Right now, Paul sat on the ground, heavy gun-fire all around him, staring down at his stomach that was cut from end to end, forcing him to hold all seven and a half pounds of his intestines in his hands, while he cried out for a medic that would never come. He tried his best to push his guts back inside of his stomach, but every time he got them inside, they would just pour back out. *He should have passed out by now*, he thought, *or one of the enemy's bullets should have put him out of his misery at least. How did this happen?* He couldn't remember. Maybe he had caught some shrapnel from an F1 grenade, or perhaps it was an RPG-6, or maybe it was one of those damn SA-2's that had gotten him. He was so used to constant mortar falling all around him at this point, Paul came to the conclusion that figuring out what had actually done him in seemed like a waste of his thoughts.

Still desperately trying to push his guts back inside, Paul tried to move past the wondering, but his mind just wouldn't let go. So he found himself lying there, soon to be just another casualty, thinking maybe it was actually friendly fire that had sealed his fate. He'd seen it happen before, more times than he cared to remember or to even think about, but until the darkness came this was what continued to fill his head, as the war continued to rage on all around him, with no pause or anyone even noticing this fallen soldier.

Where the fuck was that damn medic? All he wanted was the morphine, sweet and glorious morphine. The morphine would bring that darkness, and put an end to this endless nightmare, but the sidearm bearing the bright red cross was still nowhere to be seen. In earlier wars that bright red cross was proudly displayed right across a medic's helmet, but in this war it didn't take long for medics to figure out that their insignia doubled as a beautifully painted bullseye for enemy snipers.

Paul stopped fussing with his intestines, so they just pooled into a bloody mess in his lap, as he instead turned his attention to the harrowing war-zone all around him. *Where the fuck am I?* he thought to himself, before remembering the answer to his own question. They had gone on a late-night sweep to a thin strip of land that ran for just over forty-miles or so, that U.S. forces called Cigar Island. Paul looked around at the carnage, as their efforts had completely engulfed some remote fishing village, making it completely unrecognizable. Completely unrecognizable was sadly something Paul had grown accustomed to seeing, as countless times before they had rolled into countless tiny villages and farms with M67 Zippo tanks, and burned them completely to the ground.

Suddenly, all of the blazing sounds of war fell silent, almost as if they were sucked up with a vacuum before they were replaced by the sounds of a crying baby. The thought of seeing some newly orphaned baby crying out for a mother or a father that would never come again was more than Paul could bear, causing him to quickly close his eyes as his whole body had started to shake. The baby continued to wail, and much to Paul's horror, the cries started to get closer and closer to him. He continued to keep his eyes closed. The crying was right in front of him now, but not for long, because the sounds of war abruptly came flooding back into his ears in a hurry, drowning out the crying baby.

"You have to get up," was shouted in Paul's face, causing him to open his eyes to see the red cross on a medic's sidearm staring back at him/ "You have to keep moving," the medic continued.

"I don't think I can walk, because my intestines..." Paul replied, looking down to show his intestines sitting in his lap, only to see that his small and large intestines were no longer on the outside of his stomach. In fact, his stomach had no wound at all, leaving Paul very much perplexed, as he looked up to the medic, only to find his own face staring right back at him.

"You're fine. You have to keep going, though, or you won't be," Paul the medic said to Paul the soldier, as he lifted him up off the ground, the continuing firestorm of bullets flying all around them both, "Just keep moving, soldier!"

Paul jerked awake in a cold sweat, still sitting in that God-awful chair, the Met's broadcast long over, replaced with off-the-air static now. He quickly checked his stomach, thankfully finding no sign of his large or small intestine on the outside, before slowly getting up and heading into the bedroom to look at the empty baby crib. The leather satchel was tucked firmly under his arm.

Paul's boots, still soiled with another man's blood, made their way up 42nd street. Night had already fallen, but the lights of the storefronts of *The Deuce* burned bright, illuminating the flowing crowds of miscreants. *How could this many sinners, all just pushing toward more and more sin, be out at the same time each and every night of the week?* Paul pondered as he continued toward his own approaching sins.

Paul lit up a smoke as he moved with the flow, satchel slung over his shoulder, his eyes continually trained on the various promises of those endless sins of the flesh. He noticeably had a little more pep in his step now, flicking his spent cigarette butt toward the street, before making his way inside his own desired destination of debauchery.

At one point, New York City had nearly one hundred and fifty adult bookstores, with the largest and most famous of them all opening up in 1977. Show World Center was located on 8th Avenue, and would manage to stay open until 2018. The place was once described as *"The McDonalds of Sex'"* and was owned by Richard Basciano, who people in the neighborhood called *"The King of Porn."*

Staying open that long was far from an easy task with rent increasing across the city, along with city and state officials approving the 42nd Street Development Project in 1984. Unlike earlier attempts to clean up the city, this plan seemed to have some actual bite to it, relying on new zoning ordinances and the use of eminent domain in an attempt to wash away the clinging grit and grime in the area. Officials thought they had the teeth to get it done, but Basciano and a group of 106 other property owners in the area formed the Coalition for Free Expression and were able to tie up the efforts in lawsuit after lawsuit against the city for years.

In 1993, Rudy Guiliani was elected mayor of New York, running on a platform that specifically focused on cleaning up the city, and returning it once again to prominence. He again used strict zoning laws to force the shuttering of many adult businesses, along with implementing a 60/40 rule that required any adult book store to carry 60% of non-adult merchandise in order to stay open. Basciano and the Coalition for Free Expression once again tried to fight the changes in court, but would ultimately end up losing.

Those adult book stores that had the good-fortunes of not being located within 500 feet of a school, day care, or church, and were willing to adapt to the 60/40 rule, managed to stay open, but the others quickly faded into nothing more than distant memories.

Show World Center was one of the few survivors, and it might have stayed open past 2018, but the good ole King of Porn died in 2017, and Basciano's estate decided it was time to get out of the adult business altogether. So, when Show World Center shuttered its doors for the last time, soon to be replaced with an $80 million office building called The Hive, the nearly one hundred and fifty adult book stores was down to just nine remaining in the area at that point.

Of course, Paul knew nothing of the ill-fated, soon to be nothing more than one hundred and forty-one pieces of New York's gritty history, because all of this was still years away. But even if he had known, he wouldn't have given it much time or thought, because his focus right now was on one, and only one, adult book store.

He had barely made it through the door when he heard, "Hey, Byron!" The teller called out over her shoulder toward the room in the back, before licking her lips and nibbling on the bottom one, as her eyes fluttered toward Paul. Paul on the other hand, cautiously scanned the store, as he tightly clutched that satchel at his side.

"Yeah, whatcha need?" Byron answered, looking up from the pages of the July 1977 issue of Playboy Magazine, less than thrilled to see Paul back in his store. "Man, get yo ass —"

"Hey, it's all good, man," Paul said, cutting him off by holding up a handful of cash, and following up with, "We cool?"

Byron eyed the money as if it were his lifeblood, before nodding back at Paul. With his insatiable greed satisfied by the sight of Paul's stack of dead presidents, he put his head back into the Playboy, looking at Playmate Sondra Theodore's spread. After a moment, though, he would look up again to see Paul was now standing directly in front of him.

"Oh, this oughta be interesting," the teller said under her breath, with a mischievous smile splashed across her vivacious lips.

"Help you with somethin'?" Byron asked a noticeably apprehensive Paul, who nervously looked toward the teller, before casually spitting out, "It's... it's business."

"And my business is on these here shelves behind you, or in those sticky booths in the back," Byron replied, growing increasingly impatient with each passing moment Paul continued to take up his time.

"I...I want to buy a gun," Paul said quietly, again looking uncomfortably toward the teller, causing Byron to nod his head, before motioning for her to take a walk. Both Paul and Byron made it a point to watch her seductively walk away, before returning their attention to one another.

"A gun? Man, you are some kinda fry," Byron said, his interest genuinely peaked at this point, as Paul peeled off a few bills from his roll, and put them in Byron's palm. "What the hell does a writer need a gun for?"

"Does it matter?" Paul replied, "Just make the connection for me. All I'm asking."

"Does it...man, I don't need this shit," Byron scoffed, before once again turning to the Playboy, this time settling in to read the interview with civil rights activist and politician, Andrew Young.

Born Andrew Jackson Young Jr., Young started out in the 50's as a minister in the United Churches of Christ, and was a big believer in the teachings of Gandhi, namely his methods of nonviolent protests. Later he would become a prominent figure in the Civil Rights Movement, and at one point was Dr. Martin Luther King's assistant, before ultimately becoming one of his closest and most trusted confidants. Young would go on to be the executive director of the Southern Christian Leadership Conference, before choosing to step into politics, where he would be elected to Congress in 1972, after an initial failed attempt in 1970, representing the Atlanta, Georgia area. He would go on to be reelected in 74 and 76, during which time he was a member of the Congressional Black Caucus. But Young was just getting started. 1977 would be a big year for him, as President Jimmy Carter appointed him to be the first African-American to serve as the United States Ambassador to the United Nations. He was an inspiration to countless African Americans, just like Byron, and would continue to inspire many in the decades that would follow.

Paul, on the other hand, was stuck looking at the picture of actress Pamela Serpe on the magazine's cover, who was most known for *Girls on the Road*, *Three the Hard Way*, and 1976's *The Watts Monster*. Leave it to Playboy magazine to mix nudity in with an interview with an influential activist, all inside a cover that was graced with a middling actress. That middling actress stared back at Paul, all smiles and scantily clad in a bathing-suit, while she hugged the giant inflated playboy bunny logo. Completely flustered with the slight, Paul quickly turned his attention back to Byron, who continued to read the interview, giving no inclination he was ever going to give in unless he got what he wanted. So, Paul was ultimately left with no choice but to be the one that caved.

"Fine. I...I saw an old drunk stabbed to death last night on the subway," he reluctantly shared, causing Byron's eyes to once again come up from that magazine to meet Paul's.

"And?" Byron asked, causing Paul to look around nervously, before he shared his personal details.

"And I have a wife and a new baby to go home to at night. I...I just want to make sure that happens, is all, and the only gun I own is an old hunting rifle that I can't exactly take onto a subway," he finally replied, as he locked eyes with Byron. Mentioning his wife and daughter, personal details he initially had no intention of sharing when he walked in here, somehow managed to give him some much-needed confidence, or perhaps it was just a focused sense of purpose. Regardless of what it was, Paul made it a point for his eyes to never leave Byron's from that point on.

Byron contemplated his next move, sizing Paul up and down as he did before he eventually put out the palm of his hand and waited for Paul to line it with some more cash.

"I may know a guy," he said, his statement getting him the money in his outstretched hand, before he continued with, "I'll set it up, but it's going to take me a few days."

"Great. Thanks," Paul replied, before starting to walk away from the counter, but Bryon had other plans. He lunged forward, abruptly grabbing a hold of Paul's shirt, as he aggressively pulled him forward. Now face to face with one another, they were close enough to kiss, but Byron didn't seem like he was in a kissing mood.

"But if you fuck me on this, man, I'll –" he said to Paul, clenching his teeth, but there really was no need to finish the thought, as Paul had already put up his hands as a sign of peace.

"Yeah, I got it," Paul replied. Byron slowly let go of his shirt, and allowed Paul to head back toward the peep show booths.

"Catch you on the flip side, Jack," Byron said to him, mere seconds before Paul was in the back, and out of sight, allowing Byron to turn his attention back to his magazine. "Fuckin' weird ass cat."

Paul made his way toward the back, dropped a quarter into the change slot of the peep booth, and sat back as the dark window in front of him started to slowly come up. It was the same booth as before, and unsurprisingly, Paul was convinced it came with the same sticky residue on the floor 24/7, 365 days a year. The sticky sounds that came from his boots once again got his attention, causing him to immediately notice the dried blood stains on them, but it was a temporary focus, as the divider in front of him was still moving upwards.

Legs. Long, seductive, legs were once again the first bit of flesh before his eyes, and they were followed by the rest of the scantily clad seductress on the other side of the glass. The same dancer as before, she started to move for him, the two of them locking eyes, causing them both to smile.

Paul wondered if she recognized him. But how many guys must she see sitting in the exact spot he was sitting each day?

She moved, grinding her hips, with a level of sensual eroticism that steamed up the partition between them. Literally. She was every boy's wet dream. She was perfect in every way. And she knew it. Paul's eyes followed the soft lines of her body, as they moved to the music, the bright lights causing her skin to glisten with sweat, taking her sexual prowess to even greater heights. He looked like a lost puppy doggy as she started to take her top off just as the divider started to go down, but this time there would be no disappointment. This time there would be no unhinged rage.

This time he coolly popped more change into the slot, causing the divider to go back up, and bringing smiles to both of their faces as she continued. She seductively lost her top, but seemed flabbergasted when she looked up to see Paul writing in his notebook. She banged on the glass in outrage.

"Right. Just...just hang on a second!" Paul shouted out, holding up a finger, signaling for her to wait. She tried her best to right the ship, but her rhythm had been noticeably affected by the speed bump, her eyes clearly focused on that notebook now. "Almost done!"

She tapped her ears, and mouthed that she couldn't hear him, but he was too busy tearing out the page in the notebook, before holding it up to the glass. She stopped dancing all together, and looked at what was written: *I need your help. Please.*

She pulled back from the glass, noticeably uncomfortable now, prompting him to hold up some money for her to see. "I'll make it worth your while!" he shouted, the cash certainly getting her attention. The two of them stood frozen, just like that, with Paul holding the cash and the dancer still uncomfortable, but obviously considering the offer.

Suddenly, Paul felt disgusted. Disgusted with the money in his hand, disgusted with the cum residue underneath his boots, disgusted with where he was, and most importantly disgusted with himself. *How many times had this poor girl been propositioned just like this?* he wondered. But despite the question posed internally, he still remained frozen, still holding up the cash in his hands. He felt himself sweating now, his stomach turning, the urge to get sick finally causing him to lower the money, but there would be no puking in the booth. She had other ideas, and quickly knocked on the partition, jolting him out of his head, as she mouthed the word, "*okay,*" before holding up a finger motioning for him to wait a minute.

And that was how their relationship would start; a proposition that made them both noticeably uncomfortable, but still their paths were destined to cross. Their relationship would change Paul in ways like no other relationship ever had, or that any ever would in the future. Of course neither the dancer nor Paul knew any of this at this point, but the match had been lit, and now it was only a matter of time before the flame would ignite them both.

Paul sat in a booth in Bickford's Coffee Shop across from the dancer. Off the clock now, she was dressed like a young girl from the Midwest, her hair in pig-tails, wearing a skin-tight romper, with the short-shorts leaving little to the imagination and really showing off those never-ending legs. Paul found his mind drifting as he looked at those legs, wondering just how old she was, and guessing that at best she was eighteen, but in his gut he sadly knew better.

With the flood of tourists coming from the Midwest, countless girls just like the dancer worked the "*Minnesota Strip,*" a phrase the police used to describe a particular stretch of Eighth between 42nd and 50th street, because a great deal of the prostitutes that worked the area were believed to be runaways from Minnesota. This belief was so popular, that an article in *Time* said, "*Minneapolis police claim that up to 400 juveniles a year from the area are lost to other cities, with most of the youths winding up in prostitution in New York.*"

Maybe the dancer was one of those runaway youths, or maybe she wasn't? Paul wondered as he and the dancer sat in silence for a beat, both sizing each other up, with Paul periodically looking around at the others in the busy night spot. Eventually, he settled with the notion that where she came from, just like the countless others just like her, really didn't matter anymore, because the city already owned a part of them that they tragically could never get back. Youthful innocence is fleeting for everyone on a long enough timeline, but for the runaways that found themselves in New York City that innocence was polluted, exploited, and ultimately discarded before most of them were even old enough to vote.

"Not what I had in mind when you said we should get a drink," she finally said, looking around herself at the 24/7 coffee spot and its various patrons. She was far from the only "dancer" in the place. She nodded toward the few others that made eye-contact with her, something that wasn't lost on Paul, whose eyes were locked exclusively on her at this point. *Perhaps the nods were a silent sign of respect between them, or maybe it was a sign of mutual sadness and acceptance*, Paul thought to himself, as her eyes finally returned to him.

"Yeah, well I'm kind of just making this up as I go along at this point," Paul replied, just as the young waitress approached with her coffee pot in hand, and a thinly-veiled look of jealousy splashed across her face. She filled two cups of coffee, and the two women just stared at one another.

"Aren't you going to introduce me to your new friend, Paul?"

The dancer started to answer with, "Oh, my name is –" but Paul was quick to cut her off before she had the chance to finish.

"No. No! I...I don't want to know your name," he blurted out, before turning his attention to the waitress. "Just the coffee tonight please, Linda."

"Somehow I find that hard to believe," Linda replied, before taking one last disgusted look at the dancer, and heading off to do her coffee rounds, but not before she left them with a parting gift. "Tell your wife I say hello, Paul."

Paul just stared at her, jaw clenched, when he noticed several patrons now looking at his table. Normally, Paul could just brush the extra attention off, but there was nothing normal about tonight, nor would there be much normality in the days and nights that would follow. What Paul had in the satchel at his side would see to that inevitable and foregone fact.

"Look, you know just because I'm a dancer, and...just because I said you were cute..." the dancer said, before taking a sip of her coffee, as she took off one of her shoes, and continued with, "That doesn't mean I'm going to fuck you." She strategically started to run her foot in between his legs under the table, with a smile.

Her sudden act of sexual aggression caused Paul to look around nervously at everyone again, before gently pushing her foot away from his crotch.

"Good. That's a relief because I don't think my wife would be okay with that."

"Say it ain't so, the only good guy to ever visit *The Deuce* is sitting across from me."

She said it half seriously, half visibly disappointed, but either way, what she said caused Paul's demeanor to quickly shift.

"Hey, I'm not a good guy," he said, with some real meat behind the statement, as he lit up a cigarette, that familiar shift behind his eyes once again, as any warmth that was just on display moments ago had now been replaced with something far colder. Her statement stung in a way that not only infuriated him, but also had his head spinning with confusion. *What was wrong with her for thinking he was a nice guy?* Paul thought, as he tried to calm himself back down, so that he didn't manage to scare her away completely. *Maybe she was right*, he thought, *but maybe he didn't want to be a good guy? Maybe that was the problem, and maybe that was why this erupting internal conflict was finally bubbling to the surface?*

"No?"

She shook her head in disbelief, a smile on her face. It seemed she wasn't about to let him get by so easily with the disputed statement, having met more than her fair share of not-so-nice guys over the course of her short, but eventful, lifetime.

"No," Paul replied rather bluntly, causing her to lean across the table to get closer to him, either unable or unwilling to let this one go.

"Come on, doll. You took me to a diner." She started to get up from the table. "Like it or not, you're a nice guy, and...this is just a little too weird for me, so I'm out of here."

"Wait. Please. Just sit down," Paul pleaded, but she still hesitated, prompting him to slide the satchel across the table to her. "Open it. Carefully." Paul wasn't kidding when he said he was just making this up as he went, and now this was the only card he had left to play, and she was leaving him no choice but to play it right here, and right now. How she reacted to the satchel's contents would forever change Paul's life, one way or another, so he was sure that getting to that reaction sooner than later was certainly a good thing.

Like ripping off a Band-Aid, why prolong any incoming pain or suffering? he thought to himself, as he watched her reluctantly sink back into the booth before carefully peering inside the satchel. Her face immediately became twisted and perplexed to the point Paul immediately started to have second thoughts about showing her at all.

"Is...is that what I think it is? You know you're lucky Byron didn't catch you with this in his store, or he would have rolled you for it. Hell, half the people in here would probably do –"

Paul abruptly lunged across the table, snatching the satchel back from her, just moments before two beat cops passed their table. Truth be told, had the police stopped and searched the bag, Paul thought he had just as much of a chance of being shaken down for the contents as he did of ever going to prison.

After all, it was only five years earlier when the Knapp Commission issued a report on the city's police corruption, and in doing so they labeled two types of dirty cops. The first were known as "*Meat Eaters*" and were known for blatant and aggressive misuse of their power for their own self-gain. The second group were labelled the "*Grass Eaters*" because they would accept bribes and payoffs that came with working the job. Oftentimes it didn't take long for even honest cops to at least become part-time Grass Eaters to prove their loyalty to their fellow cops, and just as often Grass Eaters would soon find themselves crossing over to join the Meat Eaters. Frank Serpico said in 1970, when discussing the New York Police Department, that, "*Ten percent of the cops in New York City are absolutely corrupt, 10 percent are absolutely honest, and the other 80 percent – they wish they were honest.*"

Before Serpico turned the NYPD on its collective head, police corruption in the city ran rampant, with shakedowns of drug dealers, pimps, prostitutes, illegal gambling, along with cops providing protection to various legit businesses, as well as members of organized crime families.

Serpico's efforts to go public about the corruption he witnessed firsthand, along with the efforts of the Knapp Commission, would ultimately pay off when a patrolman named William R. Phillips was caught accepting a bribe from Xaviera Hollander, a madam who ran an Upper East Side brothel. Years later, Hollander would go on to share her side of the whole ordeal, and then some, when she went on to write the best-selling book, "*The Happy Hooker.*"

Once pinched, Phillips talked fast, and spilled everything on everyone, opening the door for massive changes in police policy throughout the NYPD, as well across the entire nation. Phillips, a 17-year veteran of the NYPD, would ultimately be sentenced in 1975 to 25 years to life for a murder case in 1968. He was sentenced for the deaths of a pimp and a prostitute, who prosecutors argued were killed over a failed protection payment, but Phillips swore he was framed for their murders as retaliation for turning on his fellow officers.

He studied law while incarcerated, and fought both his own case, and cases of other inmates, for nearly the entirety of the 32 years he'd end up serving, ultimately taking his own case all the way to the Supreme Court, where the ruling was upheld. But, at 77 years of age he would finally be paroled, but not before his health started to decline after a stroke and battles with cancer that ended up costing him one of his eyes.

For his own efforts, Serpico was rewarded for turning on his brothers by being shot during a drug raid two years later when the two officers who were providing his backup left him high and dry. To add insult to injury, both officers were awarded medals for saving his life even though they never even called an ambulance. He would retire after the event in 1972, with his story being told to the masses in a novel by Peter Maas, that would be adapted by screenwriters Waldo Salt and Norman Wexler for the Sidney Lumet 1973 film that starred Al Pacino in the lead role.

For all Paul knew the Knapp Commission had made the two cops who had just passed their table into that illustrous 10 percent of honest cops, but who really could tell at this point. After all, it was 1977, and the city was currently sandwiched in between the corruption that Serpico helped expose in 1970, and the 77th Precinct's "*Buddy Boys*" scandal that would happen in 1986.

The 77th Precinct was in Brooklyn, and nothing was off limits when it came to the extent cops on the beat would go to line their own pockets. They would steal the cash confiscated from drug busts, and even go so far as to pillage scenes of burglaries, taking whatever the burglars left behind. But at the height of their corruption, the crooked cops would go on to actually create their own crime scenes, which often times resulted in straight up robbing drug dealers themselves in announced, off-the-books raids that always started with the familiar radio call of "Buddy Bob" to round up the usual participants who were looking to earn a quick, and dishonest buck.

The precinct's reign of corruption would go on until Internal Affairs were able to turn Officer Henry Winter after catching him in his truck with cocaine. Winter flipped to save his own ass, with his partner and he wearing wires for almost a year, and provided more than enough for indictments on over a dozen officers, with countless others relocating to other precincts. All of the officers were found guilty, except one, who committed suicide before he was ever arrested. Winter's testimony may have initially saved him from prison, but he too would take his own life shortly thereafter at his mother's home.

Now back to Paul, the dancer, the satchel, and those cops. Clean or otherwise, once they finally passed the table, Paul immediately turned his attention back to the dancer for damage control with, "Sorry. I didn't mean to –"

"Guess I was wrong about you, darlin'," she cut him off before he could finish and her words, and the close call with the police, caused his adrenaline to kick into overdrive. In some weird way, her words of validation towards his impurity, seemed to give his wild side permission to come out and play with the rest of the misfits and deviants of the city's streets. She would soon help quiet the angel on his shoulder, while holding up a giant bullhorn for the devil on his other. Soon she would help make it so that he could streamline that wicked devil's voice into his ear, so that it could quickly move right on down into his rebellious bloodstream.

"Yeah, you haven't seen anything yet," he said, with fire in his eyes, causing her to flash a seductive smile his way, his heart practically beating out of his chest at this point. Two arsonists, from two very different walks of life, had found one another, and together they were about to set everything they touched ablaze, something that would be far from exclusive to the two of them over the course of the summer of '77 in New York City.

"Well...you said you needed my help. I'm listening," the dancer said, before taking a sip from her coffee, her eyes glued on him, and only him, the entire time.

Paul had her now, and he knew it, the realization of which caused him momentary panic, because he knew he still had to keep his cool. He still had to keep some edge, or she would see him for what he really was, a phony who was clearly faking it, at least until he could make it. He didn't know it at the time, and perhaps he never would actually know, but in a lot of the ways, the dancer was also nothing more than a phony, trapped in a world that only ever really saw her as one, and only one, thing.

"Good. Because if we do this right, you can quit Byron's fucking store," Paul replied, as he took another look around at the other patrons, his eyes once again landing on the cops who were just finishing paying their bill before they hit the door.

They wore uniforms, just like he had when he served, and Paul guessed that much like he had during the war, the officers at least initially signed on to serve for the greater good. But now those badges represented something different to him. Paul knew those badges had the potential to stand between him, and doing what he needed to do to provide for his baby, and just like when he was in the trenches, he now knew as he watched them leave that he would be both willing, and able, to do whatever was necessary to come out on top of any run-ins with the NYPD. Ultimately he hoped it would never come to that, because just like the countless "enemy" soldiers he had killed, Paul thought about how they too had children they were just trying to get home to in one piece. This thought seemed to echo inside his very core, as he continued to watch the two police officers until they were completely out of sight, allowing him to once again return his attention to the stunning beauty sitting across from him.

"But why me?" that stunning beauty asked, as she finished her coffee, before reaching over to take what was left of his cup.

It was an honest question, and frankly one Paul had not given much thought to until just now, but she of course would never know that, because it didn't take him very long at all to find an honest and valid answer. He watched her drinking what was left of his coffee, before finally answering once the cup was completely dry.

"Because you live in a world I know nothing about. Yet."

Paul sat, and really relished the "yet" part of his answer, as he watched her reach out, taking the dying cigarette from him, and finishing it completely.

"You want to live in it…or just work in it?"

They locked eyes with one another. *Those eyes were truly something else*, Paul thought to himself, as he found himself lost in them for a moment, while she impatiently waited for his reply. New York was full of beautiful women, full of beautiful eyes, but she had something more. There was something in those eyes, deep inside those eyes, deep inside her very soul, that had Paul thinking that in another life, she could have easily been a movie star. The thought brought with it some sadness, though, because this wasn't another life. This was the hand that she had been dealt, and here she was, the "dancer" with movie star eyes, that were locked onto his own, still waiting for him to reply.

"Is there a difference?" Paul finally blurted out, his response immediately causing her to shake her head "no."

"No...not after a while," she said, sure of herself, and for good reason.

"Okay. Any more questions, or can we get started?" Paul asked, as he lit up another cigarette, ready to fill his head with something, anything, other than the thoughts that brought on all of this sadness he was suddenly finding really hard to shake.

"Just one. You have any idea what you're doing?" the dancer asked, once again taking his cigarette from him, but this time only taking a drag, before handing it back.

"Guess we're about to see," Paul replied, throwing down some change for their coffees, before getting up, the satchel thrown over his shoulder.

"Let's go," he continued, as together they walked from their booth, while Paul eyed the many faces that were littered throughout the spot, on their way out into what was left of the dwindling night.

> *Junkies, pimps, freaks, hoods, squares, blue-collars, white-collars, pigs. The giant melting pot under the night's sky. I used to think of them all as...different, but now...now they were all the same to me. Now I just saw them all as...customers. My customers.*

———

Fresh twenty-dollar bill after twenty-dollar bill were placed down onto the bar with some real vigor. "And that should cover my tab, and this..." Paul said, as he peeled off another twenty from his clip, and placed it on top of the others, "...this should cover a few rounds of celebratory drinks, my dear."

Vicky stood on the other side of the bar, looking as if she had seen a ghost.

"What? Say something already," Paul pleaded, as her eyes started to well up with tears, and her entire fragile frame started to shake.

Seeing her that way, with those tears starting to stream down her face like an old and rusted pipe that suddenly burst, surprisingly hit him hard, and caused his own eyes to start to water.

"Wait, what are you...this is supposed to be a happy moment, Vicky."

"I am happy, asshole," she replied, leaning over the bar, grabbing him by the face, and kissing him on the cheek. "I knew they would buy your manuscript. Always knew you had it in you."

Paul went to speak, but she was already off and running, as she shouted out to the few regulars in the joint, "Paul sold his manuscript!"

The scattered few amongst the place barely replied with a collective grunt or groan.

"Hey, am I talking to myself here?!" she yelled out. This at least seemed to wake the bunch up enough for them to put together a half-assed collective cheer. "Yeah well, guess we have to grade on a scale around here, all things considered," she said, before she turned her attention back to the man of the hour, still beaming for him, her excitement sincere and genuine.

"Look, Vicky, I'm glad you're so happy for me, but –" Paul said, but she put her fingers over his lips, causing him to reluctantly clam up like a good school boy who was just waiting to be disciplined.

"Shhhh, my beautiful friend. For once I wish you'd at least play the writer stereotype, and be a fucking introvert," Vicky said, as she took him by the hand, and brought him over to the jukebox. "I'm almost afraid to ask. Any requests?"

Paul looked at her, soaking in all of her genuine beauty that at this point, tragically, only he still saw in the old broad, before replying, "Ladies' choice."

His response caused a smile to creep across her face. Messed up teeth aside, the smile was nothing but warm and heartfelt, and something Paul had desperately pined for his entire life.

Vicky pushed the buttons on the jukebox, making her selection, before turning to him and saying, "I'm so proud of you."

Paul pulled her close to him as the two began to dance their dance, and he whispered in her ear, "Thank you, Vicky." One could call it the calm before the storm as the two danced, because the world seemed to stand still, albeit only for a few minutes, and those few minutes were sacred to the both of them.

Later that night, Paul made his way through the massive glass doorway of an upscale New York apartment building, still carrying the leather satchel, and was almost immediately met by a gruff doorman wearing a spiffy uniform.

"Evening. How can I help you?" The doorman asked, as he did little to hide the fact that he was eyeing Paul up and down while waiting for a response.

"Hey, I'm trying to get to..." Paul started to reply, as he fished out a tiny piece of paper with the hand written address written across it.

"Suite 1800?" the doorman asked, as his prying eyes landed specifically on the leather satchel, making Paul pull it closer to his body. "They keep calling about you."

"What?" Paul asked, as the doorman came out from behind his station, and led hesitant Paul to the elevator. "What do you mean they keep calling about me?"

'Just come with me," was the only answer Paul was going to get, at least for the moment, as the doorman turned a key that granted them both access to the elevator. They stepped inside the claustrophobic-inducing box where another key was turned, and the button marked PH was pressed, prompting the doors to close. "My night has been filled with phone calls from the suite asking if you've arrived yet," the doorman finally said, as the elevator started its ascension.

"If I've... but you don't even know my –" was Paul's partially dumbfounded answer, but he was quickly cut off by the big man standing next to him, who was taking up so much of the extremely tiny space.

"Your name?" the doorman said, as he stifled his laughter. "What difference does that make?"

Paul quickly became flustered, and wasn't shy about expressing it at the doorman's expense. "What difference does...what's to keep anyone from just coming in the building, and coming up here if you...if you don't even ask for identification or –"

Again the doorman cut him off. "For one..." He pulled open his uniform jacket to reveal he had a gun tucked into his waistband. "And secondly, I don't need to see your fucking ID Mr. Stephenson, because I'm very good at what I do." The elevator stopped, and the doors opened. "Now, let's make this quick, so that I can get back to the door, to make sure that..."—he stepped out of the elevator with a shit-eating-grin on his face—"...not just anybody comes in the building."

He motioned for Paul to step out of the elevator. "Arms up, legs apart," Paul did as he was told, and the doorman carefully frisked him. "Am I going to find anything?" He asked, and the question brought with it Paul's internal, and self-focused, ire.

"Nope. Haven't got that part squared away yet," Paul replied, as the doorman finished with another dubious smile, shaking his head in disbelief, before buzzing the doorbell to suite 1800. And then they waited. Neither man made eye contact with the other, but just stared at the door that remained closed, with the muffled sounds of music seeping out through the cracks. The song was something familiar to Paul, but the door was too thick for him to make out what exactly was playing. The door being thick, though, was something Paul certainly noted to himself, as the waiting continued.

The buzzing from the other side of the door brought with it a great ass in panties, as it moved toward the door, and finally opened it to reveal the doorman and Paul impatiently waiting out in the hallway.

"Good evening, madam. Mr. Stephenson has arrived, and he's clean," the doorman said to the owner of that great ass.

"Thank you, dear," the dancer said as she took Paul by the hand, and brought him inside the posh space, closing the door, with the doorman craning his neck to get one last look at that great ass before the closed door killed the view.

"You live here?" Paul asked. The place was easily a hundred times the size of Paul's place, and screamed old-money, with an architectural design consisting of ridiculous high ceilings and an outlandish 360-degree view of the city that never sleeps. The high-rise's architectural layout may have been old and "classy," but clearly it was furnished and decorated by an interior designer with a more modern flair, one that straddled a fine line between elegance and flamboyance. The muddled mixture of the two different worlds collided inside the ten thousand square foot penthouse, which was something that was very much in line with the city and its inhabitants at the time. All of this was normally something that Paul himself would have noted, being as observant as he was, but his eyes were not on the apartment at all at the moment.

"Sometimes. Come on," the dancer replied, trying to lead him into the next room, but he had already physically dug in his heels.

"What's wrong?" she asked, looking back at him, while he was conflicted as to how, or even if, he should respond to the question.

"Why are you dressed like that?" Paul eventually asked, as he continued to stare at his scantily-clad host, causing her to seductively smile before moving in close to him.

"Like what?" she whispered in her ear, before gently resting her tongue in between her top and bottom lip, just long enough to purposely moisten them. Paul was obviously torn as to how to react to any of this, all while she continued to stay too close to him, her beautifully, and recently moistened, lips still only inches from his ear and neck.

"I...I thought I was here for business," Paul finally got out, causing her to lean in even closer, gently nibbling on his ear, and leading him to close his eyes, frozen in a raging storm of nerves and swelling lust.

"You are. All of this is business. You're going to have to trust me, if we're going to be working together, babydoll," she said, and just like that, she practically bounced away from him, and headed into the next room. "Come on then. In here!"

Paul took a much-needed moment to catch his breath and to steady the ship in the storm, finally looking around the space now and taking in all of its grandeur. "You coming or not?" the dancer playfully called out. He clearly didn't fit in here, but there was no turning back now, so he headed to the next room, and once through that door frame, Paul would find himself in what amounted to an entirely new world.

Paul was immediately greeted by more beautiful women, lots and lots of stunningly beautiful women, and each and every one of them was dressed in only their bras and panties.

The beautiful women moved about the space, but most of their actions were central to their participation in the cutting, weighing, and bagging copious amounts of cocaine.

Erythroxylon coca, otherwise known as the coca plant, had been chewed by the natives of Western South America for generations for everything from religious ceremonies, to just getting through the rigors of arduous work. It was believed that chewing the leaf was able to provide them with needed energy in place of proper quantities of proper food and water, especially at higher altitudes.

Needless to say, this fun little tidbit caught the attention of Europeans, who immediately tried to extract the chemical ingredient that was providing the stimulant back in the 19th century. Their efforts were rewarded in the 1880's, and the extracted stimulant was used both recreationally—initially in tonic form—as well as for various medical practices and applications, most notably as an effective local anesthetic.

The more common use of the drug is manufactured, sold, and distributed in a white powdered form that is often adulterated (or cut) with another ingredient, oftentimes to a 50/50 ratio. Cocaine is cut with everything from lactose and glucose, to straight up baby laxatives. Despite the added boost to bathroom visits, cocaine continually carries a high price, along with an exotic high, making it a status drug over the years.

For some historical perspective and context around the world that Paul was stepping into, the street price in 1977 was between $60 and $100 a gram. Three and half grams, or an 1/8 of an ounce is better known on the streets as an "eight ball." 28.3 grams is an ounce, or an "O," with 62 grams better known as simply "sixty two." An eighth of a kilo, 125 grams or 4.4 ounces, is called a "big eight," followed by a "quarter kilo," "half kilo,"" three quarters of a kilo," and finally 1000 grams, or 35.27 ounces, simply known as "one kilo."

When cocaine first entered the U.S., most often through a seaport, it was packed into massive sacks with individual packed kilograms inside. These shipments usually came in with heavy weight, oftentimes in metric tons. One metric ton of cocaine weighed 1,000 kilograms, but that weight was usually stepped on, or cut, at least once, often numerous times, before it hit the hand of the consumer. So, even if it was only stepped on once, the weight was doubled, so one metric ton of cocaine would be worth upwards of two hundred million dollars in 1977.

Of course, Paul knew none of this, as his experience with drugs up to this point was the overly liberal amounts of marijuana he had smoked while in Vietnam, along with a tiny dabble with some high-grade dope. Heroin was all around him during his tour, as one fifth of all enlisted soldiers who fought in the war had become addicted at one point or another, but Paul had managed to dodge that bullet, his only taste coming after having the misfortunes of watching his superior officer die in his arms, crying out for his mother before taking his last breath. Thankfully a simple taste allowed him to check out just long enough, without getting its claws into him long term. But cocaine was a far different high, and for Paul it was a whole different story. Paul was a cocaine virgin, but the captain of the football team was coming on strong, so it was only a matter of time at this point.

"So, this is the wondrous Paul that I've heard so much about, huh?" Chevy Blinko, an incredibly flamboyant middle-aged man who was wearing eye-shadow

and an ill-fitting wig, said as he made his way over to them. Paul thought it was a safe assumption that Chevy had lost his cocaine virginity a lifetime ago.

"Told you you'd love him," the dancer replied, as Chevy stared, completely awestruck with Paul, so much so it was making him noticeably uncomfortable.

"Oh, I do. I so do," Chevy said, paying no attention to Paul's discomfort or growing impatience.

"Great. You love me, and you know my name. So is this where we do the intros?" Paul said in a hurry, his eyes once again drifting toward all the beautiful women throughout the room, before his attention moved to all of the cocaine. Why did this guy even need what was in the satchel? What Paul was carrying paled in comparison to the massive weight in the room. Of course, there were answers to both of these questions, even though Paul would never know them personally.

Chevy came from money, and grew up in the Hamptons in a very well-to-do family with a wealthy lineage that went back for countless generations. He went to the finest prep schools, and moved in the kind of social circles that were "invite only." Of course those invitations came from the last name on one's birth certificate, a last name Chevy was quick to change once he reached the legal age.

Apparently growing up in a prominent family wasn't always a path paved in gold for a flamboyantly gay man who was coming into his own, and who was tired of spending so long in the closet. Of course, there were others, and Chevy often found himself either giving or receiving a blow job in an actual closet at many of the various luxurious dinner parties that made up his youth, but those other boys would never give up the silver spoon in their mouths to put a cock in it out in the open. Chevy knew this from the get-go, but he rode it out for as long as it lasted, with the irony of the use of an actual closet for their sexual encounters never lost on him.

Chevalier Jeffrey Rosen eventually found himself on the outside looking in on those social circles, and by the time he was a freshman in high school, he was spending more time in various holding cells across New York city than he was at those posh and bloated dinner parties. By the time his class-mates were accepting their diplomas and heading off to some preordained Ivy League college, Chevy had built himself up quite the rap-sheet. He had been hauled in for petty theft, prostitution, armed robbery, aggravated assault, and of course, his personal favorite—possession of a control substance. He would gleefully add the "with intent to distribute" to his favorite criminal activity years later, but at that point he was just using to get high like everyone else.

All of it, though, the entire rap-sheet, was just his way of taking the edge off. The moment the clock struck midnight on his eighteenth birthday, he was flush from a very generous trust fund, so he didn't actually need to do any of the things he got busted doing, but Chevy never did anything because he had to in life. He did things because he wanted to, and even more importantly perhaps, because he could.

Chevy Jeffrey Rosen didn't need Paul, or what he was carrying in his satchel, any more than he needed the guy who used to come around before him. He also didn't need to kill the guy who used to come around before Paul did either, but he did it because he wanted to, and even more importantly, perhaps, because he could. Of course, it didn't help the guy's cause any that he was skimming off the top, and either didn't care enough to hide it much, or perhaps he was foolish enough to think Chevy would never notice. But Chevy didn't have to notice, because he paid people who would, and who ultimately did.

Chevy also didn't have to kill the guy himself, but again, he didn't do any-thing because he had to, so literally gutting the man like a fish with a switch-blade fell into the "because he wanted to, and because he could" category. Chevy was a lot of things in life, but above all else he was a certifiable psycho, ready and able to go off the deep end at any moment in time.

Chevy didn't need Paul, or the contents of that satchel, not by a long shot, but after the gutting of the fish there was a job opening in the operation, and the dancer was one of the few people that honestly had Chevy's ear. It didn't hurt Paul's cause that he was both attractive and in a committed relationship that left him sexually repressed and blue-balled. All that pent up and unsat-isfied sexual energy subconsciously oozed out of Paul, and it was something that both the dancer and Chevy picked up the moment they laid eyes on him.

"How you feeling, Paul?" Chevy said, as he gently turned Paul's chin with a single finger, so that the two were now facing one another. Personal space was never a high priority for a man like Chevy Blinko.

"Like I'm in the dark here, and severely overdressed for the occasion."

"Well, a new wardrobe certainly wouldn't hurt you, dear, but you can keep your clothes on if that's what you're asking," Chevy said, as he bit his lip, still staring into Paul's eyes.

"Paul, meet Chevy Blinko," the dancer said, before taking a seat next to some of the other girls, as she started to help with the process, leaving the two of them to their own demise.

"Let's go talk some business," Chevy said. Paul reluctantly followed him into another room, but not before he gave the dancer one more parting look. It was a look which she graciously returned, along adding that infectious and seductive smile for good measure.

The next room, a full-fledged bar with a bartender included, was just another piece of the luxurious place. The bartender greeted them, pouring two green shots and lighting each one on fire before pushing them toward the duo. Chevy blew both flames out, and passed one of the shot glasses to Paul. "Drink up, sweetheart," he said, but Paul pushed the shot away.

"Business first," Paul said, as he put the leather satchel on the bar. "Then we drink to celebrate." But Chevy just stared at him, causing the bartender to back away in apparent self-preservation, while making Paul increasingly nervous. Chevy eventually broke the stare, then flipped open a switchblade knife, causing the bartender to actually flinch. "Hey take it easy, man. I'll drink the fucking shot," Paul managed to get out, before Chevy said his piece.

"Did you know that Vincent Van Gogh drank so much absinthe..." Chevy said, as he pounded one of the shots, before picking up Paul's shot, "...that it contributed to him cutting his own fucking ear off." He downed the second shot, nodding to the bartender for another round, to which Chevy once again blew out both flames after they were lit.

"Oscar Wilde said that after the first glass of absinthe you see things as you wish they were," Paul said, as he downed one of the new shots, before reaching for the second one and downing it as well. "...and after the second, he said you see them as they are not."

"And what about after the third?" Chevy asked, as he motioned for the bartender for a third round.

"He said you see things as they really are," Paul replied, as Chevy blew out both flames, before he took one of the shot glasses, and passed the second to Paul, as they eyed one another. "And that is the most horrible thing in the world."

Chevy pointed the switchblade at Paul for an uneasy beat, before using it to point toward the leather satchel. "Let's see it," he said, prompting Paul to open it up, and allowing a peek inside, before Chevy abruptly plunged the knife into the satchel.

"Shit!" Paul said, nearly dying from a heart attack. Chevy pulled out some white snow on the blade, and snorted some of it right off the tip of the knife.

"Shit is right. That's some grade-A shit you've got there, sweetheart," Chevy said, as he dabbed his finger in it, and swirled it around his gums. "It hasn't even been cut yet."

"So do we have a deal?" Paul asked, still eyeing the blade, as Chevy put it down on the bar, and raised his shot glass.

"You bring me this pure stuff, my girls will step on it, and package it, and I'll handle the distribution. Deal?"

"Deal."

"Good!" Chevy raised his glass. "To seeing things as they really are," he said.

They clinked glasses, and each drank their respective shot.

***

Paul, now dressed in flared, high-waisted trousers with a front crease and patch pocket, a long-sleeve dress shirt with a wide pointed collar, and platform shoes, stared at a line of people that wrapped around the block, all waiting to get inside a building that was built in 1927. It was the San Carlo Opera House back in those days. These people were not waiting to get into any opera, though.

"I feel stupid dressed like this," Paul said, to the dancer at his side.

"But you look great, and even more importantly, you look like you belong," she said, as she led the way, the two of them walking right passed the velvet rope, straight through the blacked-out doors, and into a whole other world.

Wall-to-wall with celebrities, like Cher, Calvin Klein, Andy Warhol, Michael Jackson, and Truman Capote, Studio 54 was a veritable who's who of the social world. The place was filled with loud music and bright colors that fueled the night as sex lingered in the air, and much to Paul's delight, drugs were everywhere.

The brainchild of two businessmen, Steve Rubell and Ian Schrager, the duo initially rented just a portion of 254 West 54th Street in 1976, with the full business opening up on April 26th, 1977. To say it was an immediate success from the get-go would be a massive understatement. No one would ever know for sure the actual number, but estimates put the club's first year gross revenues close to seven million dollars, with the place continuing to flourish until December of the next year when it was raided by federal agents. The raid ended with Ian Schrager being arrested for possession of cocaine. It would be only the first of numerous legal issues the club's owners would face over the course of the next few years.

In June of 1979, both Rubell and Schrager would be charged with tax evasion, obstruction of justice, and conspiracy, with the year ending with IRS agents raiding the club after an article in New York magazine in November included interviews with disgruntled former employees. The duo would hire celebrity attorney Roy Cohen, but still would end up being sentenced to federal prison time for tax evasion. They would go out in style, of course, throwing a legendary, star-studded, all-night party the night of February 3rd and into the morning of the 4th, before heading off to serve their three-and-a-half year prison terms. They'd end up giving up names, and serving only thirteen months for doing so, but then they would sell the club in November 1980 to hotel mogul Mark Fleischman for 4.75 million. Fleischman would own the club until 1986, when it would close its doors permanently, just nine years after it opened.

The club's lifespan was short-lived, but those nine years were eventful years, and just like the club he loved, Steve Rubell would burn out young, ultimately succumbing to complications from AIDS on July 25th in 1989. But Paul experienced the club in its infancy, long before any of those troubles or tragedies.

"Come on!" the dancer said, as she pushed into the crowd, Paul struggling to keep up with her movement.

"Where are we going?" Paul asked, while he barely avoided a young woman walking by on a horse. Yes... a fucking horse, the sight of which had Paul questioning if he was dreaming at this point, but that was pretty much Studio 54 in a nutshell. Club attendees who were fortunate enough to get through the front doors were gifted access to a dreamland while they were wide awake.

"To the party," she replied, shouting over the excess of swelling noise, because they could barely hear one another as they continued to push through the crowds.

"Aren't we already here?" he replied, as he started to get overwhelmed with everything, causing the room to feel like it was literally whirling around him.

"Well, aren't you the cutest," she said, as she smiled at him, playfully pinching his cheek, before she once again continued on through the mass of sweat-soaked bodies, all grinding against one another.

"What? I'm not following," Paul shouted out as he scurried to catch up.

"This is just an appetizer. Something to whet your appetite," she replied, just as a completely nude model, covered from head-to-toe in glitter, smiled at him as they passed. "Real party is in the basement."

"Consider it soaked," he said, more to himself than to her, as his attention quickly became fixated on a woman who was leading a handful of handsome boys around on leashes. "Yeah, can't wait to see this basement."

With the main floor overflowing with legendary levels of decadency and overindulgence, the basement was ripe with an ungodly amount of depravity and debauchery. But no one here was complaining.

Actual mattresses populated the place, all occupied with people in various stages of fucking. Some were couples, others were whole groups. "Okay, seriously? Where the hell are we?" Paul asked, as he tried to take it all in. Nothing was left to the imagination here, because if you could imagine it, this was the place you could actually do it.

"Heaven. Hell. Depends on who you ask, I guess," she replied, as they stopped at a long table, where a completely nude woman was meticulously laying out perfectly dispensed lines of cocaine. "But I thought you'd like to see your product was being put to good use." There were dozens of the lines, all the same length, and width. It was a thing of art in a lot of ways. "Owners hired her to do nothing but set up these lines."

"Every day?" he asked in sheer amazement, causing her to laugh.

"Don't be crazy. Every hour, babydoll. Speaking of which, you need to see your supplier, because they need more," the dancer said, her words making him noticeably uncomfortable.

"Oh well...this was more of a one-time thing," he said, causing her to shake her head "no," as she ran her fingertips across the skin of his forearm.

"Oh, babydoll...it doesn't work that way," she replied, mere seconds before another girl to his left tried to hand him a rolled-up dollar bill.

"No thank you," Paul said, putting his hand up to keep the bill away from him, but the dancer had no problem taking it instead.

"Come on...let's celebrate," she said, trying to hand him the bill, but ultimately getting the same negating response.

"You go and enjoy yourself. I'll just watch," Paul said. She leaned in close to him again and she kissed him on the cheek.

"Fine. Your loss," she said, before taking her place at the table along with dozens of VIPs, as they collectively all partook in unison.

With each line she snorted, the sights and sounds of the legendary club's basement quickly became a blur, as the night raged on. From that point on a lot of Paul's life would become a blur, and a lot of his nights would rage on, too.

MANHATTAN: Tuesday July 12th, 1977

PAUL SAT ALONE IN THE back of a cab, gazing longingly out the window, as night slowly became early morning. The rising sun glistened off of wet city streets, proudly announcing the start of a new day.

"Long night?" the cab driver, your average-Joe in his 40s, asked, but Paul didn't respond, instead choosing to keep staring out the window. "Not interested in small talk. I get it. I didn't mean to be nosy or nothing. Just keeps me awake behind the wheel."

"So we've established we're both tired," Paul finally chimed in, turning away from the window, but still paying no attention to the driver. He opened up his notebook and started to write instead. "So, why not punch your timecard, and call it a day?"

"Because sleep doesn't put food on the table," the driver answered, taking a sip of something from a thermos.

"No, I guess it doesn't," Paul said, finally looking up, the two sharing a look through the rearview mirror. "Kids?"

"You bet. Seven of 'em," the cabbie replied.

"Jesus…" Paul's gaze shifted from the rearview, to a pinned photo of the driver and his large family on the dashboard. "Seven. Trying for a baseball team?"

"At this point, we couldn't be any worse than the fucking Mets." That at least got Paul to chuckle before he went back to writing in his notebook.

"How about you? You got kids?"

"One. And that's enough."

Paul looked down at the blank page in his notebook. He wanted to write. He had so much he wanted to say. The words should have been overflowing, spilling out from his mind and soul like a geyser. The words should have been flooding that blank page, and the countless ones that followed. But the page would remain bone dry for the moment, and Paul was oddly at peace with that fact, at least for the time being.

"Then you know that driving my ass all around the fuckin' boroughs and cleaning up all the piss, blood, puke, cum, whatever's in that backseat, is just a means to an end. You do what you gotta do. For your kids. Right?"

It was a timely statement and question, but Paul didn't reply, although the sentiment was one that was already resonating with him long before he ever even stepped foot into the man's cab. A little over six months ago the bundle that was a little over nine pounds came along and forever made the answer to his question a definitive "yes."

Paul had certainly seen a lot over the course of his thirty-nine years, enough probably to fill two lifetimes, but witnessing the birth of his child was the ultimate of ultimates. It was the most awesome of events, one to which there never was, and never would be, a legitimate peer. Paul knew this the moment Lily drew fresh oxygen into her tiny lungs, before using it to exhale her first newborn cry. The high pitch wailing was sweeter than the greatest of love songs, and those infantile notes of birth immediately brought him to his knees, the tears practically leaping from his eyes.

Back in his tiny apartment, Paul picked up baby Lily. She was all smiles, cooing and eyes-wide, as he brought her up to his face. He kissed her forehead, a proud and loving moment between father and daughter, as her mother lay fast asleep to the world. Paul pulled her up to his chest, holding her in his arms now, and gently rocking his body to create a soothing, rhythmic motion. As they both settled into the movement, he quietly whispered something to her, something that was to her and to her alone.

The leather satchel, now filled with money, sat open on Mr. Mackey's cluttered desk.

"Needless to say, I'm impressed."

He was brimming with greed as he looked at the fruits of Paul's labors. Paul sat across from him as the old man poured two glasses of high-end scotch, before passing one to Paul and keeping one for himself.

"Cheers."

They clinked glasses, before each taking a sip, the editor's eyes never leaving Paul throughout their exchange.

"What?" Paul asked, feeling Mr. Mackey's eyes on him.

"How'd you do it?"

"I don't follow."

His editor smiled, before pouring himself another drink, and motioning for Paul to slide his glass over for a refill. One thing Paul learned pretty quickly in this new world he was rocketing through was that it was never too early to celebrate. *It wasn't even noon yet, but apparently large stacks of cash had made Mr. Mackey thirsty*, Paul thought, as he watched the scotch barely have time to settle in the glass, before it was already half way down the man's throat.

"Come on. The weight I gave you usually takes my guys on the street a whole week to move," Mr. Mackey said. Paul went to answer honestly, but he quickly caught himself. Another thing that Paul was learning pretty quickly was that speaking honestly was like speaking in tongues in this business.

"Just lucky I guess," Paul finally settled on for an answer.

"I've known you for years, and not once have I taken you to be someone who's lucky, Paul."

"Yeah well...guess things are changing for me lately," Paul replied, as he finished the drink in his hand, before sliding the glass away from him.

"I guess so," Mr. Mackey said, as he started to pour them another round before Paul interrupted him. "I'm good on the drinks. I just need more stuff. A lot more." Mr. Mackey just sat there, with his big bulging eyes still locked on Paul, but not saying a word. "Look if you can't do it that's fine, but –"

"No...no...I can certainly do it," Mr. Mackey said, cutting him off before he could finish. "Just didn't think you'd want to go down this road, is all."

"Yeah well...like I said, things are changing for me lately."

The two stared at one another some more, before Mr. Mackey finally went to his safe, and took to opening it up.

"I have some here, but the amount of weight I think you're talking about, I'm going to have to get elsewhere," Mr. Mackey said, as he turned around, both hands filled with cocaine. "Won't take me long. You'll have the rest by tonight."

Paul packed up the new product, and that's when he got a really good look at Mr. Mackey's eyes. His pupils were the size of small saucers, and they took up the majority of his entire eyeball. It was called mydriasis, and was usually caused by a non-physiological cause like some kind of trauma, certain underlying diseases, and of course certain drug use. Mr. Mackey was sure as shit high on his own supply, and seeing his pupils had Paul's mind drifting off toward a distant memory of his childhood.

Paul was twelve, maybe thirteen, when he had come home from school one day and his mother was looking at his eyes like he was looking at Mr. Mackey's right now. He remembered her forcefully grabbing him by the arm, hard enough to leave fingertip-sized bruises, while she held him still to investigate his pupils further. The inquisition started the moment he had walked through the front door. It continued through the car ride to the hospital, into the thirty minutes or so of waiting in the waiting room, before it finally came to a merciful end when the two of them were in front of a doctor.

The entire time Paul had stuck to his story. He told her he had no idea why his pupils were so large. This did not satisfy her, nor did it squash the questions that just kept coming. He told her that he was not on drugs. This did not satisfy her. She continued to insist otherwise. She was sure he was on drugs, and was hell bent on proving it, hence the visit to the doctors.

Paul stuck to his story when they were in front of the doctor too, who had his own set of questions, while he examined the pupils in question. Paul told him he had no idea why his pupils were so large. Paul told him that he was not on drugs. It was easy for Paul to stick to his story, because his story was the truth, no matter how much his mother insisted otherwise, and after the mini examination, the doctor agreed. Even this did not satisfy his mother, though, who asked about doing an actual drug test so that they could be totally sure about it.

It was at this point that the doctor took his mother outside into the hallway to speak in private. Paul couldn't hear what was being said through the closed door, but when his mother came in red-faced and seeing red, he had a pretty good idea.

The inquisition had died a slow and painful death, but it was finally rotting away six feet under by the time they were driving home in the car. Her face remained red the entire ride, but she never said another word about it. She hated being wrong, perhaps more than anything in life, and it was clear to him, even at an early age, that she had no idea how to deal with it when it happened. Paul would quickly learn that when your parental figure doesn't know how to express or even rationalize being wrong, it made for one hell of an uneasy and imbalanced childhood.

Paul had no doubt his mother loved him, especially in the earlier days of his childhood, but at some point, she started to change. Her transformation consisted of little, subtle things at first, but eventually she would emerge from her midlife cocoon with a full-blown undiagnosed bipolar disorder.

Paul and his brother tried to tell the extended family about their mother's behavior, but for reasons that neither would ever truly understand, their pleas fell on deaf ears for years. Of course, at that age, years living with a single mother who was bipolar seemed more like a lifetime. They were just kids, gradually growing into their own, and on top of all of the other stresses that life threw children at their ages, they had to deal with not ever knowing which version of their mother was in front of them.

Some nights they would go to bed with her being the epitome of unconditional maternal love, kissing them on the forehead, and telling them to "have sweet dreams," only to wake to some crazy monster who had gone completely sideways while they slept. Each and every day, they never knew what to expect, and because of it, they were always on edge, always waiting for the other shoe to fall. It was a crushing introduction to approaching adulthood, and Paul knew the days of living at home with his mother were numbered.

He couldn't get out of there fast enough, which was something his mother could never comprehend. Even after he packed up in the dead of the night to move in to an apartment with some friends from school, she seemed shocked at the concept of him even wanting to vacate, but Paul had made up his mind that he had to turn the pages in his life, with the new pages being void of this mother character all-together. So that's how it went. His life, page after page, chapter after chapter, and even book after book went on for years without her completely, almost as if she never even existed, at least until she reappeared in the chapter that saw her pass away.

By then Paul didn't even know how to feel about the woman who had given birth to him. He knew he was supposed to feel sadness, but really all he felt was an emptiness. A part of him thought he should feel some guilt for being estranged from her for so many years, and a part of him honestly did, but ultimately, the thing he felt most about his mother's passing was that emptiness.

Despite his vastly uneven and oftentimes tumultuous childhood, Paul knew his veins still pumped with the lifeblood of both of his parents, and with that lifeblood also came a whole slew of unavoidable hereditary traits. One of those unavoidable traits was an addictive personality, a trait that was only exacerbated by the childhood trauma. Up 'til now it had laid somewhat dormant, but it was still there nonetheless, festering just beneath the surface.

Time ticked by, and it continued to lay in wait, a festering abscess that was just now starting to puss up, working its way toward being septic. It was only a matter of time before he was in full-blown septic shock.

A massive line was being snorted inside of a Studio 54 bathroom stall. When it was finished, Paul lifted his head, rubbing his nose feverishly.

"There you go, babydoll," the dancer said, before she kissed him. This time it wasn't on his cheek. It started off soft and unsure at first, but soon they were all over one another. In between kisses, she managed to say, "My name is Stephanie."

Like I said before, it takes time, perseverance, and patience to build oneself into a full-blown addict.

Their clothes came flying off, hot skin pressed against hot skin, and soon they found themselves entangled in the throes of passion. Raw... animalistic... passion. His lips moved from hers, to her ear, then down her neck where he continued to kiss, lick, and even bite. Paul continued to work his way downward, pulling her top down from her shoulders, exposing her perfect breasts, as he continued to kiss and taste her soft flesh. She, in turn, dug her nails into his back, prompting him to grab her wrists, pulling her arms above her head, and slamming her up against the wall, before returning to working his mouth over the entirety of body.

"Is that all ya got?" she asked, with fire in her eyes, and a thinly-veiled smile starting to show at the corners of her mouth.

"Not even close," Paul whispered softly into her ear, as he quickly turned her around, before tearing her panties down from under her mini skirt. Pressing up against her from behind, he pulled at her hair, turning her face so that they could kiss, while moans of pleasure started to build over the continuing music that endlessly echoed throughout the place.

Not long afterwards, the duo would continue their explorations of one another, in a more toned-down manner, on the *Studio 54* dance floor.

Now I had my taste.

The full-blown disco experience was in full effect, countless bodies all around them, everyone moving to the music. The sea of movement engulfed them, holding them tightly in a hypnotic state. It was a rush, a full-body high that started before, and ended long after, any synthetic high that was coursing through their veins.

People can be addicted to anything really. Drugs, booze, gambling, sex...hell during my two tours I ran into more than a few who were without a doubt addicted to death.

The dancer put a piece of acid in her mouth, before offering him a piece, which he quickly ingested.

> *I've always known I had an addictive personality, even from a young age. Maybe I'm genetically predisposed to addiction. Who knows.*

All smiles as they again locked lips, while the disco raged on, overindulgence floating all around them.

> *What I do know is, there will be no more gradual initiations for me, because...*

Paul once again sat in the graffiti-riddled subway car, writing in his notebook.

> *...now...I am...a full-blown addict.*

The leather satchel rested on the seat next to him, cautiously tucked under his elbow for protection.

> *So what was I addicted to? Hell at this point, to steal a line from Johnny Strabler, Marlon Brando's character in The Wild One... "whaddya got?"*

A woman's scream jolted Paul's attention from the page, to the other end of the car. The group of hoods that stabbed the drunk were once again up to no good.

"Come on, baby...we just wanna little taste of that sugar," one of the hoodlums said crudely. Tonight they were taking out their devious desires on a young woman who had the misfortunes of getting on the wrong train at the wrong time.

"Please, just...just leave me alone," she pleaded, but the hoods all laughed, enjoying each and every moment of her growing panic. The few other unfortunates on the train all cringed, but did nothing more than look away, including Paul. "Please. Just stop!" she continued to plead, as she tried to push one of them away, but he easily overpowered her, and started to grope her chest. "Get off of me!"

The train came to a scheduled stop, and as soon as the doors opened every other rider quickly exited, leaving only the young woman, the hoods, and Paul.

"Someone hel—"

She didn't get to finish screaming, because the main hood put his hand over her mouth, just as the train started back up again.

"I told you bitch, we just want a little taste," the main hood said, opening the switchblade he used to kill the drunk, and flashing it before her eyes. A moment later he closed the blade, but still kept one hand over her mouth, muffling her screams as tears started to trickle down both her cheeks. "Let's see whatcha got." He started to run his free hand up her thigh, getting closer and closer to in between her legs, as she continued to struggle in vain to break free from his grasp.

Paul desperately tried to keep his head down, failing miserably at being anything even remotely close to a good Samaritan, as the horrors continued. With one hand between her legs now, the hoodlum took his other hand off of her mouth, and literally ripped her shirt downward from the neckline, exposing her bare breasts underneath, and causing her to frantically scream.

"You like that don't you?" her predator asked, as she continued to scream in vain, sobbing uncontrollably now, as he started to unbuckle his pants.

"Leave her alone," Paul finally blurted out, causing the hood to smile before turning around to face Paul.

"You're a dead motherfucker."

He didn't get to finish, because as soon as he turned around he was smashed in the face by Paul's fist which sent him reeling backwards onto the seats as his partners in crime quickly moved toward Paul.

"Are you okay?" Paul asked the young woman, but she didn't answer, as she desperately tried to cover up, while quickly moving to the other side of the train.

The other hoods collectively lunged at Paul, prompting him to punch one before going on the defensive and dodging the second. Back on the offensive, as soon as he dodged the aggression, he sent the avoided hood to the ground with a thud from a vicious elbow to the back of the man's head.

As Paul continued with the others, the main hoodlum opened up his knife again and looked to get in on the action while shouting, "I'm going to fucking kill you!"

But what happened next was a thing of beauty. Violent...unrelenting... beauty, that continued at an outrageous pace. A dance of improvised aggression, it was an outlet of sorts for Paul's ever-building rage. A flurry of fists and feet flew forward. Skin was bruised. Blood was splattered. Bodies were smashed up against the windows, cracking the glass and crunching bones in the process. Paul could certainly handle himself, but with the numbers against him, even his military background didn't prevent him from receiving his own fair share of the beating.

The whole time, the young woman continued to cower, as the violent exchange happened all around her in the enclosed space, at least until the train made another stop, and she managed to successfully flee out the opened doors.

But she was not the only one.

"Fuuuuck!" Paul screamed out, as the main hoodlum retreated, but not before grabbing Paul's leather satchel and exiting, mere seconds before the doors closed in Paul's face. "Noooo!"

Completely helpless, he smashed his hands on the doors, but the train continued on, and Paul's distraction quickly led to the sharp blade of a knife being plunged into his side! "You fuckin' piece of –"

Paul quickly retaliated, pulling the knife, before smashing the unfortunate hood in the face, over and over, and over, and over again with his fists!

Gruesome amounts of blood splattered all over Paul's face as he literally beat the man's head into a pulp, before finally relenting out of sheer exhaustion. Sinking to the ground and trying to catch his breath, he looked over at the remaining hoods, who appropriately looked as if they wanted nothing to do with him at this point.

The train slowed for another scheduled stop, and the hoods quickly fled, leaving Paul alone with the dead body. Paul wiped the blood from his face and slowly stood up, lost in thought as he stared at the mess he had made, before eventually getting off at the next stop.

━

On December 1st, 1969 CBS News picked up a live feed from Roger Mudd, who was covering the draft lottery at the Selective Service Headquarters. There were 366 plastic capsules, each one holding a birth date and dumped into a glass container, each waiting to be drawn out, and the corresponding birth date to be assigned to a number, starting with 001.

September 14th was the first birth date drawn from the container by New York Congressman, Alexander Pirnie, who at the time was the ranking GOP on the House Armed Service Committee. Pirnie had been invited to draw the first capsule by Selective Service Director, General Lewis B. Hershey, who had held the position for nearly thirty years, and who had been new to the position in 1940, the last time the United States had held a war-time draft.

Hershey wasn't exactly beloved at this point, and often found himself the target of anti-war protestors, particularly on college campuses, where he was often picketed, booed, and even pelted with eggs for his efforts, which brought him to issue a recommendation to local draft boards that any man who interfered with military recruitment on a college campus should have their draft status reclassified immediately. By this time Hershey was on his way out as Selective Service Director, but much to the dismay of the growing voices of dissent towards him, he was still allowed to oversee this draft, much like he had nearly thirty years earlier. He would refuse to retire, though, and ended up being involuntarily retired in 1973.

Paul and Valentina watched the broadcast on his 1967 Zenith console color television, just like the other millions of other young men and their families would watch on their own sets, or listen to the radio broadcasts of the live event, but there was one thing that was for certain that night for each and every one of those young men. Everyone who had tuned in was just praying that their birth date wouldn't be drawn too soon, with their fates to be forever sealed by the simple luck of the draw. That luck of the draw was actually something President Nixon was keenly aware of, as he insisted that young people of draft age actually be involved in the draft process itself, so after the initial pick by the Republican politician, selected youths stepped forward with each picking a handful of capsules.

Both Paul and Valentina thought it was an empty token, a sad attempt to try to appease countless young men and their loved ones who would soon be leaving American soil, never to return again. What neither of them, or anyone else really for that matter, could imagine would be the toll that those who actually returned would endure and carry home to those same loved one.

Apparently, Paul and Valentina weren't alone in their assessment, though, as four of the five youths actually declined to participate, sharing the same feeling that they were nothing more than pawns in a game for the Nixon administration. Paul couldn't help but think just how painfully out of place the term luck of the draw was in this ordeal.

More than 800,000 draft eligible men between the ages of 19 to 26, who didn't already have their draft status resolved in one form or another already, would learn what their participation in the war would look like that fateful night. Unlike previous drafts, it went from youngest to oldest when it came time to report after your number was drawn, so for someone who was 19 and had a low number, their fate was sealed relatively quickly in 1970.

With lottery numbers of those 19-year-olds being called at a ridiculous rate, those with low numbers could be given an order to report for a physical examination letter and have that physical as early as February or March. Those without a valid reason for deferment from that group could find themselves in active duty by May of 1970. Those fortunate enough to get a deferment could do so if they could prove they were a student in college, and in good standing toward their way toward a degree, or apparently they could be from the wealthy elite and have a medical deferment from bone spurs.

Those in the unfortunate crowd, Paul being one of them, were classified as 1-A and subject immediately for service. Paul, and his fellow lowlifes, those whose daddy didn't sugar-coat life for them, fell into the lottery number spectrum of 001 to 215. Paul was born on December 29th making his number 016. He wasn't in college. His parents weren't rich. Both Paul and Valentina knew Paul was going to war if he passed his physical, which he did on February 24, 1970. Paul was going to war, and everything he and Valentina had built between the two of them during their short time together would have to be put on hold. Perhaps it helped that they didn't know one another that well, all things considered, or perhaps it helped that all of Paul's friends were being called over too, but regardless, the pause was oddly accepted by both of them when they knew it was inevitable. They could of course run, together, to Canada or Mexico perhaps, but neither Paul nor Valentina even so much as broached the subject.

His number was called, and he was a patriot, so he would serve, and he would serve to the best of his ability. He never lost sleep over this fact, and she only loved him more for his definitive and clearly patriotic take on being called into action. This was the kind of guy she could see herself with, not just for a short-time fling, but for the long haul. Paul would never know it, but the night they knew his draft status would ever solidify her love for him. In her eyes, he was the perfect, and safest, guy she had ever met, in that they could/should/would have children together, and Paul would keep all of them safe. Paul wasn't her first choice. Paul probably wasn't her last choice, but Paul was a safe choice. At this point in her life, Valentina needed safe choices, albeit ones that she might never see again.

For Paul this whole ordeal was surreal up until the point it wasn't. He loved the fact he had a beautiful gal at home who was waiting for him. He loved the fact he was serving the country that he was raised to love and cherish. He loved that he being pushed into the most uber--masculine place a man could be pushed into, and he loved that a part of him was scared out of his fucking mind, but the other part of him was beyond exhilarated.

No one ever talks about the idea of being green-lit to kill another human being. It's unconscionable to talk about such things in common circles, but Paul was about to find himself in a whole new set of circles. These circles were made up of mommas' boys, that Paul knew out the gate wouldn't last long, all the way to straight-up, hardcore, stone-cold killers, who relished the fact that what they were being called to do, and what they were going to do, would not only be okayed, but they could actually go home as heroes at some point.

Paul saw a momma's boy killed literally seconds the moment they stepped off the plane. This one in particular was hard to watch, as he was a tightly wound kid from Illinois, a boy who had dreamed of a bland, but safe, life as the veterinarian of the small town he'd called home since the day he was born. But there was nothing bland about the bullet that shattered half his skull, somewhat numbing him to his shrinking reality, as he continued to press on, as if he hadn't been hit at all. This Illinois boy pushed forward like a good soldier, with half of his head blown away, but somehow his brainstem was still operating just enough for him to carry out the basic movement of walking forward, his gun still in his hand, truly no different than a chicken with its head cut off.

This horror show went on for only a few minutes, but it seemed much longer because everything seems to slow down when you're in the thick of it. You'd think it'd be the exact opposite, and Paul guessed that for some it probably did, but not for him, and if there were ever a time when he wished it had this would have been it. The Illinois boy turned to say something to the others, but his tongue didn't seem to work, so nothing but some bloody drool dripped down from his lips, and Paul guessed that was when he realized that all was not well.

The look on his face even seemed off. He wasn't scared, or mad even, but instead he seemed to just laugh, with the side of his face that still existed struggling to twist into something that at least remotely resembled a smile. Perhaps that was part of his brain finally shutting down, or perhaps someone has mercifully stuck him with some morphine without Paul noticing, but either way, he was grinning and laughing as he stood there just looking at the others, enemy fire still ripping all around them, with no sign of letting up anytime soon.

Paul just wanted it to end. He wanted to stop being shot at. He wanted the boy to stop smiling. He wanted the boy to stop laughing. He wanted the war to be over, and for his body to be back entangled with Valentina's, their sweaty bodies writhing against one another until they both peaked, but above all else in that particular moment, Paul really just wished the boy would hurry up and die, and he knew deep down inside he wasn't the only one who was hoping and even praying for that end.

Prayers are nice. They certainly serve a purpose, and Paul certainly said his fair share of them during the war, but those particular prayers seemed to fall on deaf ears, because that Illinois boy just kept standing there, still smiling and laughing as bullets continued to flying all around him, with half his fucking face missing. Again, this went on only for a few minutes, and even though Paul and the others found themselves busy returning fire, and bunkering down for safety, the Illinois boy seemed to live for another two lifetimes.

When he finally died, it wasn't from the aftermath of his injuries. It wasn't because of more enemy fire. It wasn't because of any prayers from Paul, or from prayers from any of the other poor saps who were also unfortunate enough to have their numbers drawn. The boy died, because Paul put him out of his fucking misery, just like the poor boy would have done for assumingly countless animals who needed to be put down had he actually ever lived to realize his dream job as a veterinarian. One clean shot straight between the boy's eyes put an end to that horridly unnatural laughter, and ended the tour of one of many who should have never had to serve in the first place.

Again, no one ever talks about the idea of being green-lit to kill another human being, and they sure as hell never talked about mercy killings. The Illinois boy would return home a hero, a man who served his country and served it well, and no one would ever know otherwise. Why should they, Paul had thought since the day he pulled the trigger, and every single day afterward. When it was done it was done, too late for second guessing, but Paul justified it then, and still believed it even now, by hoping that someone would have had the fucking balls and heart to do the same thing for him had he been in that boy's shoes.

———

The doorway between the two neon signs: 25 Cents Peep Shows, Books & Magazines on one, and 25 Cents Live Nude Girls, 8mm Films Novelties on the other, opened and the dancer exited as she said her goodbyes. "See you later, Byron."

"Goodnight, Foxy," Byron hollered out from the distance.

She lit up a cigarette, and started to make her way down 42nd Street. Her beautiful stems covered up with a long coat now, but she was still breathtaking. Her looks didn't go unnoticed either, turning the heads of practically everyone she passed, men... and women alike.

She couldn't help but smile at the attention, but the smile quickly faded from her face, replaced with a look of sheer terror, when someone abruptly grabbed her and pulled her into the shadows of a dark alleyway. Her screams were muffled by a hand over her mouth, but even still, she was not willing to go down without a fight. So she kicked and flailed about, at least until she heard, "Shhh...easy! Easy. It's me!"

That was when settled down, and that's when Paul let her go.

"Paul, what the hell are you –?" she said, stopping when she saw his blood-soaked shirt. "Are you okay? What the hell happened to you?!"

Paul abruptly shushed her again, as his eyes went wide as two police officers passed by the alleyway. Lucky for him they kept going without ever noticing anything.

"What is going on? Talk to me," the dancer said as soon as they were out of sight.

"I could probably get the short version out before passing out, but if it's just the same to you, I could really use some help right now," Paul replied, his eyes still focused on where the police had just passed.

"Of course. Let's get you to the hospital," she said, as she tried to help him to walk.

"No!" Paul barked, as he grabbed her forcefully by the arm. "No hospital."

"Listen, Paul, that looks really –"

"I said no hospital!" he said, letting go of her arm. "Sorry. I...I didn't mean to grab your arm so hard. Please..."

She looked at him with those movie star eyes of hers, contemplating what to do next. This was surprisingly far from the first time she had seen this much blood on a person. Perhaps it was par for the profession, or perhaps it was just that New York City was a hotbed for violence during the 1970's, but that same year the dancer had witnessed the aftermath of a twelve-year-old prostitute falling from the 10th floor of the Markwell, a dingy hotel on 49th just west of Broadway, and landing face first on the sidewalk down below.

The dancer was at the Markwell Hotel too that night, and she was familiar, friends even, with the young girl, although she honestly had no idea she was only twelve. But no one that worked or visited the "*Minnesota Strip*" had any idea she was only twelve, for that matter.

The young girl was known as "Shortie" because of her small stature, and quickly became a known regular around the shady part of 8th Avenue, in between 40th and 50th Street. She was all of 5' 2", barely over a hundred pounds, and in just two short months prior to her death, she was arrested eleven times in the midtown area for loitering for the purpose of prostitution. She had been running away from the housing projects she called home on the regular by that point, and quickly became one of the countless souls the city swallowed up whole.

It was around 8 pm on that fateful night when the dancer stood staring at the young girl's practically nude body lying motionless on the hard concrete, while copious amounts of blood oozed out from underneath her tiny frame. She was sure the young girl was dead, and that her pimp had thrown her out of the tenth story window. The young girl wasn't dead, though, at least not yet.

Despite all of that blood that continued to pool around her, and despite the fact she remained completely motionless, the young girl would be alive when the paramedics finally arrived. She was alive in the clinical sense of the word, but never fully became lucid enough to tell the police what had happened, or to ask for her mother to be called.

So she laid there alone in her hospital bed, completely forgotten by the world around her already, even at the tragically young age of twelve. No one would visit her while she was laid up in the hospital, and eventually after four days of unconscious fighting to sustain her life, she ultimately succumbed to her injuries.

To add insult to injury, it took the police more than eight months to identify her, and to notify her mother, because during her arrests she never carried any form ID so that she could give a fictitious name and address. It wouldn't be until after a tip from other prostitutes that the authorities were able to put a real name to the poor girl's body, at which point her mother was contacted, the fate of her little girl finally no longer a painful mystery.

Now the dancer could add Paul's bloody ordeal to the one about the twelve-year-old prostitute, their stories just two of many that she had witnessed firsthand in her own troubled, but still somewhat nubile lifetime.

"Okay, I know a place we can go to get you cleaned up."

━━━

Phony early-American prints decorated the putrid, aqua-colored walls of the dimly lit, and sparsely furnished, shithole of a room in the Hotel Belmore.

"Here," the dancer said, giving Paul a bottle of cheap booze. Paul took a giant swig directly from the open bottle, before handing it back to the dancer, who remained a fixture at his bedside, at least for the moment. "Better?"

"I've been through worse," Paul said, as a needle pierced into flesh, pulling one loop of thread after another, thanks to the ER nurse stitching him up.

"That you have," the nurse chimed in. "Vietnam?"

"Yes, ma'am," Paul replied, as she gently touched the old bullet wounds on his back.

"Well, whoever stitched you up did an incredible job. I hope you thanked him," the nurse said, her statement having a noticeable, and immediate, effect on him.

"He was just a kid who…" Paul was off somewhere else now, as the horrific sounds of war flooded his ears, overwhelming his present being for a brief moment, before, he added, "…never made it home." The sounds were eventually muted, and he abruptly crashed back to reality.

"I'm sorry," the nurse said, real sympathy in her eyes.

"Yeah. Me too," Paul said, thankful for those sympathetic eyes.

"So is he going to be okay?" the dancer asked.

"He's lucky. They didn't hit any organs."

She finished the stitching, and took to dressing the wound, before finally packing up her portable medical kit.

"It was an accident," Paul nervously said, causing the nurse to shake her head with a smile.

"Hey, whatever story you want to tell yourself is fine by me."

The dancer greased the gal's hand with a few crisp hundred-dollar bills. "Thank you for helping him."

"He's not in the clear yet. He needs to rest. Keep the wound clean. Change the bandages regularly. First sign of infection, he'll need antibiotics."

"He's in good hands," the dancer said, gently running her fingers through his hair, as the nurse exited the room, leaving the two of them alone.

"Okay. Help me up," Paul said, and much to her surprise and horror, he was 100 percent serious about trying to get up.

"What? You need to –"

"Rest. Right. I heard her. But I'm in trouble."

"How bad?" Paul just looked at her, not wanting to answer. "Paul?"

"I...I killed someone. And that might not even be the worst of my problems," Paul finally said, his words hitting her hard and heavy.

"Jesus, Paul, what are –"

"I'll handle it," Paul interrupted, as he started toward the door, but stopped when she called out to him.

"Am *I* in danger?" she asked, real fear in those beautiful movie star eyes.

"I don't think so, but for now, why don't you stay here," Paul replied, before trying to leave again.

"I can't. I have a shift in an hour." That quickly put another pause on his exit.

"No. Stay here," he said, but she adamantly shook her head "no."

"Byron will kill me, Paul."

"Fuck, Byron! Why do you even need to work there anymore anyway?" Paul said, as he moved back to her, so that they were face-to-face now. "With the money we just made, you don't have to dance for that asshole anymore."

"It's complicated. Byron's been looking out for me since I was fourteen," she sheepishly said, unable to look him in the eyes while she said it.

"What are you saying?" Paul asked, his jaw tightening, while a look of disgust found its way onto his face.

"I ran away from home, and I...I didn't exactly have a whole lotta options," the dancer replied, still unable to look him in the eyes.

"So what...he was like your pimp?"

"Yeah, Paul, Byron was my pimp. And I fucked him. I fucked a lotta guys. Is that what you want to hear?" she snapped, somewhere between tears and boiling rage.

"Just stay here," Paul pleaded.

"He was good to me!"

"You were just a kid, Stephanie!"

"A kid who was a junkie. I was a mess, needle in my arm, until he took me in. Haven't touched that shit since."

"And then he pimped you out? Yeah, he's a real fucking hero."

"Oh, who the fuck are you to judge?! I did what I had to do," she said, tears streaming down her face now.

"Just...stay here, until I get back. Do not go to work."

"Or what, Paul?"

"Promise me," he said, before he leaned in and kissed her passionately on the lips. She resisted at first, but eventually relented. "Promise me."

She hesitated, but eventually gave in with: "Alright. Fine."

"Say it," Paul said, as he wiped the tears from her eyes.

"Okay. I...I promise I won't leave this room," she said, and with that Paul turned and quickly exited.

MANHATTAN: Wednesday July 13th, 1977

PAUL, HIS FACE STILL SCREAMING of the tale of his recent altercation and noticeably still favoring his wound, sat uncomfortably across from his editor.
Mr. Mackey just stared at him in silence for what seemed like an eternity.

"Look, Mr. Mackey, I can..." Paul tried to explain, but Mr. Mackey held
up his hand, signaling for Paul to stop. This only brought on more uncomfortable silence between them.

"I'm just at a loss as to what exactly you're expecting me to do with this
news," Mr. Mackey finally said, getting up from his desk to pour himself a
drink. He didn't offer one to Paul, and quickly downed the one he poured
from himself, before he poured himself a refill.

"I...I'm just here to...to ask for a little time," Paul said. "I promise you, I
can fix this."

"I think you may have the wrong idea about me, Paul," Mr. Mackey said,
as he sat back in his chair with a sigh, before continuing, "Did you know that
I've been married for nearly forty years?"

"No I didn't. Congratulations. That's quite the –"

Mr. Mackey stopped him again by holding up his hand. "We've known
each other since grade school. Came from the same neighborhood. Went
to the same church every Sunday. Our families were close. Friendly even,

which made it that much harder to not have my wife's father live long enough to walk her down the aisle when we got married," Mr. Mackey stood up, his mind off elsewhere now, completely lost in the continuing memory. "You see...two years before we got hitched, I crushed his fucking skull with a baseball bat. The piece of shit cried. Sobbed even before I hit him."

He moved from around the desk now, sitting on the edge of it to be closer to Paul, but he continued without ever looking directly at him. "After the first crack at his skull he was drooling, and blood and snot were coming out of his nose. After the second crack, he actually pissed and shit himself. But you know... all I could think of the whole time I was slamming the bat down on top of him, over and over and over and over again was..." He finally turned his gaze directly to Paul, their eyes meeting. "...I wished I'd killed the abusive prick years earlier."

"Why are you telling me this, Mr. Mackey?"

"I'm telling you it, because I wanted you to know that I did what I had to... to protect my wife that day, and I've continued to do so every day since. And it's my hope that you too are willing to do what needs to be done to protect your own wife, Paul."

"My wife?" Paul asked warily.

"Yes. Your wife," Mr. Mackey replied, before laughing, making all of this even more uncomfortable than it already was for Paul. "Has she been spending so much time at her parents place up in Rochester that you've forgotten you were married? Or is it that you've been spending so much time with that whore dancer with the tight little body, that it's fucked with your marital memory?"

Paul nervously shifted in his chair, and understandably so, as Mr. Mackey has picked up a baseball bat from somewhere amongst the clutter now, admiring it as he gripped it in his hands.

"No. I haven't forgotten about my wife," was all Paul was able to muster at that point.

"Well, that's good. You have until tomorrow afternoon. When I come into my office at noon sharp, you better be here with my money," Mr. Mackey said, prompting Paul to stand up and quickly head for the door to leave, but not before Mr. Mackey got in a few more parting words. "Because I'd hate to leave that little baby of yours without her mother, Paul."

Paul's jaw clenched, as he reluctantly bit his tongue before making his exit, leaving Mr. Mackey alone with that baseball bat.

He just stared at it in his hands for a moment, before returning it back to the clutter from which it came. His hands were used to holding a baseball bat, and for reasons that didn't always involve smashing open his would-be father-in-law's skull back in 1934.

In 1934, Riley Mackey was just another sixteen-year-old growing up in the Bronx, the oldest of four children. Riley's mother was a high school English teacher, and even though his father came from Irish descent he was trusted to help run one of mob boss Frank Costello's gambling parlors. But 1934 ended up being a bad year for those joints, and for the subsequent employment for Riley's father. Then New York Mayor Fiorello La Guardia ordered a series of raids on the parlors across the city, which resulted in damage to over a thousand slot machines.

After that Riley's father had a hard time holding down any kind of steady employment, and although he was far from a violent man by nature, he found himself once again picking up the various muscle jobs that had earned him Costello's trust in the first place, just to make ends meet.

On more than one occasion, those jobs required a few persuasive swings of a baseball bat.

Riley was never privy to the actual sights and sounds of any of these persuasive conversations, but he certainly heard the whisperings about it from the neighborhood kids.

Sometimes the whispers were quite loud, making it harder and harder for anyone to argue against there at least being a subconscious melting of both parents' influence on him as a young man, and even more so in his future activities and profession(s).

Riley was more than just studious in school. He excelled at heights that surprised even his intellectual mother at times, and the two would forever bond on being well read and their love affairs with literature. He also excelled in sports, particularly baseball, where he was a superstar at James Monroe High School—and when push came to shove, Riley could more than handle himself with the baseball bat when a conversation just wasn't enough.

As a sophomore in high school, Riley Mackey batted .602 with 19 home runs and 76 RBIs, while also going 12-2 with a 0.77 ERA and 124 strikeouts on the mound. Needless to say, his stats caught the attention of professional scouts, and naturally Riley thought that it was only a matter of time before he was playing in the majors. He also thought his soon-to-be wife's father was a good, God-fearing Catholic man. Riley wound up going 0 for 2 on those two thoughts, and he ended up spending two court-appointed years in the Tryon School For Boys, a facility for juvenile delinquents in upstate New York, just outside of Albany.

There would be no Major League Baseball career for Mr. Mackey. In fact, he would never play baseball again. There was also no high school graduation for him, but at no point did he not think all of it was worth it, because there was also no more inappropriate touching between the supposed God-fearing

Catholic and his teen daughter.

When Mr. Mackey told Paul his story, he left off one not-so-minor detail involving what happened to his wife's father in between the vicious baseball bat blows to his head. Mr. Mackey's soon-to-be wife was present during the whole ordeal, and she wasn't exactly a passive observer either.

Somewhere in between the drooling, the blood and snot that were coming out of the man's nose after the first crack to his skull, and the pissing and shitting that came with the second crack, his daughter got her revenge for years of abuse and she focused that revenge on the one body part that had stolen her innocence back when she was too young to even understand what was happening. With each swing of the baseball bat Riley Mackey was sure he was saving her from the monster in her life, and clearly he was, but plunging a kitchen steak knife repeatedly into his penis and testicles would prove to be some real primal therapeutic shit that she took for herself before everything was all said and done. When she was finished, the monster's crotch looked like a bloody mess of shredded flesh, no real defining characteristic left of what the bloody void was before her vengeance. The son of bitch deserved every bit of it.

The sexual abuse started back when she was too small for vaginal penetration so he had resorted to sodomy. Every moment the two of them were alone became the stuff that makes up nightmares, and she was barely out of diapers at that point. The one who was supposed to protect her from the slings and arrows of the world was too busy violating her instead. He actually beat her when she got her first period, because after that moment, it limited where he was able to finish, but even then he showed little regard for anything other than his own sick and twisted wants and needs.

She'd had two abortions before she was even in high school, the second of which caused enough scarring inside her that she was no longer able to have any children. The incestuous rape continued all the way up until the night before he was killed.

On second thought, the son of a bitched deserved worse.

The abuse, and his soon-to-be wife's testimony at trial, kept Riley Mackey from being tried as an adult, and was the reason why he was able to walk out of the Tryon School for Boys two days after he turned eighteen. They were married a week-and-a-half later, just the two of them and the Justice of the Peace, because his parents could never understand why he had given everything for her and her own mother absolutely refused to believe the sexual abuse allegations. They were both okay with it just being the two of them, though, because they knew the past was the past and that moving forward each other was all that they would ever need in this world. They both understood that life wasn't always going to go according to plan, or desire even, but no matter what, you do whatever you have to do for the ones you love, even when it's not always the easiest thing to do.

Paul knew all about this concept of love and sacrifice, as he begged and pleaded with Valentina just to listen to him. He was once again dressed like how we first met him, bomber jacket and all. He was frantically throwing clothes into a suitcase as the baby cried nearby.

"It's only for a few days!"

"And why exactly can't I go to my parents?"

Valentina was standing in the doorway and looking at him incredulously, holding their crying baby in her arms. Paul didn't expect this to be easy, but he also knew he didn't exactly have the time to be subtle, or even tactful.

"I don't have time to explain. You just can't, baby," he finally said, before returning to throwing more clothes into the suitcase.

"You're being ridiculous, Paul!" She wasn't exactly screaming, but she didn't have to, because Paul could see she was physically shaking at that point. He had known her for seven years now, and in those seven years they had certainly gone through a lot together. Seeing him off to war certainly was taxing, and giving birth to their child was monumental, but through both those events, Valentina always had a certain reserve on the surface. There was no reserve here. Paul had never seen her this rattled. Ever.

"Just do what I say, Valentina."

He finished with the packing and quickly zipped up the luggage as the baby continued to cry. From a distance, one would think the whole scene was stolen directly from some made-for-tv Lifetime movie, because it was so overwrought and melodramatic. But this wasn't a movie, and neither Paul nor his young family had the liberty of watching from a distance. Melodramatic or not, this was the hand that they had been dealt, and as far as Paul was concerned he was dealing with it accordingly.

"Where? Where the hell do you want me to go?" she asked, as she continued unsuccessfully to try to soothe their crying baby.

"Anywhere but here, or your parents."

Paul looked at them both with sympathetic eyes. Things weren't great between them, and they hadn't been for so long, but in the moment, there was no question for Paul whether or not he still loved his wife.

"You're scaring me."

Her eyes pleaded with him now. Paul slowly moved over to his wife and daughter, trying to hold it together emotionally, as he kissed them both on their foreheads, closing his eyes and lingering for a few seconds on Valentina's kiss in order to take in her scent.

"I'm not trying to scare you."

"Well, you're doing a lousy job then. You're out all hours of the night, we barely see you as it is, and now you come home with your face all bruised up from lord knows what, and you spring this on me?"

It all started to come apart for her at this point.

"I'm sorry. Please, just –"

"Just give me a minute!" she shouted, cutting him off. She was shaking even more now, fighting back the tears that insisted on coming, and prompting him to reach out. But she wasn't having any of it.

"Don't touch me! Just...don't."

"Okay. I'm sorry."

He backed away from her to give her some space, as she took to once again trying to sooth the baby, who has started to really wail at this point.

"Shhh...it's okay. It's okay. Shhhh." Gently rocking her child back and forth, the baby slowly stared to calm down, and the crying subsided. At least for the baby. "I've been trying so hard to hold it all together, but now...when I look at you, it's...it's like I'm not even looking at the same person anymore."

"I know. I'm just going through some stuff right now, and –"

"No. This has been going on for a long time now," she said, cutting him off, and cutting him to his core in the process.

"I know. I'm just...lost, and I guess I'm constantly looking for something, but I have no idea what that something is," Paul said, looking on helplessly as the tears streamed down his wife's face.

"You know, most days it seems like I don't even exist to you, and...and I don't know if it's ever going to get better," she said through those tears, causing Paul to hesitate, choosing his words carefully before finally speaking again.

"I...I don't know either."

She nodded her head as she tried to wipe her eyes, without waking the baby in her arms. "At least we found something we can both agree on. I'll go to my cousins."

"Thank you," Paul said, as he picked up the suitcase and moved it toward the doorway. "I'll get you a cab." He went to walk past her, but she physically stopped him by blocking his path with her body.

"Paul?"

"Yeah?"

"Have you given up? On...on us?" she asked, causing Paul to shake his head "no," as his own eyes started to well up.

"I know it's hard for you to see because it's hard for me to see. But...I'm not done fighting," he said, as his tears started to fall before they eventually kissed, both their lips and falling tears meeting one another in a much-needed soft and gentle moment.

Paul couldn't remember the last time he had actually cried, he thought to himself, while still wrapped up in that loving kiss. He didn't specifically try not to cry. He wasn't some fake macho guy, who thought crying was for the weak, because he had seen far too many who were actually strong and brave cry to think that way. Paul couldn't remember the last time he cried because Paul had gone numb up.

Was he starting to feel again? Was this what really living felt like? Was this how it was supposed to be?

Paul clearly had a bunch of questions in front of him now, but no answers. At least not yet.

Paul met his wife, Valentina, a little more than seven years prior, when they were both working dead-end jobs at a trendy restaurant on the Upper East Side. Paul got the job right out of high school and quickly managed to work his way up from an hourly cashier to the night-shift manager. Valentina, on the other hand, was the day-time pastry chef, which didn't exactly make it easier for them to even cross paths—let alone to fall in lust, and eventually to fall in love, but that's exactly what eventually happened. It happened, and not long after, Paul's number was called by the Vietnam War Selective Service Lottery in 1970.

For the first three months after Valentina was hired, she'd start her days at six in the morning and would be long gone before Paul would punch in at three. The closest he ever got to her was eating the leftover pastries for the day as he closed up at night, grateful that the customer's hadn't caught on to how great the pastries were now as opposed to how average, at best, they were with the prior pastry chef. So, he would reap the rewards of their ignorance, usually in the form of a brownie and/or an assortment of various cookies, as he counted the cash drawers each night and filled out the deposit slip for the next day's drop. Eventually news would travel amongst the regulars that the pastries were no longer the usual bland affair that they had once been, and Paul's score would become smaller and smaller each night, until eventually nothing left became the new norm.

Aside from her prowess with various sweets and goodies, whispers about Valentina for other reason soon started to permeate among the male staffers, as she was certainly something to look at. Her ass in particular became legendary, as the back-of-house in the restaurant had loose uniform restrictions and Valentina's choice of clothing usually involved a pair of light washed, elephant Bells—tight, high-waisted bell bottom jeans that really accentuated her tight little ass. But her ass wasn't the only thing that became legendary amongst her male coworkers, and when Paul inquired about her to the day manager that had hired her and who had worked with her before, he was specifically told she had fuck-me-eyes that would make him think she was into him.

The caution continued with Paul being told not to take those fuck-me-eyes too seriously, because that's just how she looked at everyone. So, Paul had been warned, and then some, but it wouldn't matter.

When the restaurant's manager took some time off to go to some hippie festival from August 15th through the 18th,1969 on some farmland in White Lake, in upstate New York, Paul took over the day shift, and met Valentina for the first time in person at 6:38 on a Monday morning. Coming in nearly forty minutes late for her shift, which was something she apparently did often but always got away with because she was damn good at her job, and because she looked damn good in those hip hugger jeans. Of course, the first thing Paul saw wasn't her ass in those jeans, though. She smiled at him, and said hello as she came through the door, startled to see a new face for a moment. That gave Paul just long enough to see those legendary eyes before she turned and quickly put on her apron and went to work. It was a brief moment, seconds really, but it was more than enough.

Apparently that little hippie festival turned out to be a big thing called Woodstock, and apparently the restaurant's manager was wrong about his advice of staying clear of those misleading eyes, because Paul and Valentina couldn't keep their hands off of one another after that day. Outside of work, she would leave her parent's place in Alphabet City, an impoverished neighborhood made up predominantly of Puerto Ricans, and jump on the subway to head over to the apartment that they would both call home, eventually, to hook up as often as possible. During work, they would look for any and every opportunity to make out, with the most likely of spots happening over the course of a few seconds in the walk-in cooler—just long enough to get their fix before they could finish what they started back at his place later.

Eventually, lust bore the fruits of genuine feelings, and Paul found himself wanting more between them than the animalistic sexual encounters that made up their relationship up until that point. He finally asked her out on an official date, and the two went to dinner and a movie, with Paul doing his best to wine and dine the woman who had his heart—first eating at the legendary *21 Club* behind the iconic wrought-iron gates at 21 West 52nd Street, then going to see Butch Cassidy and the Sundance Kid. The movie opened in New York on September 24th, 1969 in just two theaters in New York before expanding nationwide the following week. Paul took Valentina to a screening at the Sutton Theater at 205 E. 57th, which would be ultimately torn down in 2005 and replaced with condos.

At dinner at the legendary upscale restaurant that had been around since the end of prohibition, Paul felt famished and ordered the 21 Burger. But Valentina said she wasn't feeling all that well, chalking it up to nerves, and settled on just ordering a salad, which bothered Paul at first but he quickly let it go. He had such big plans and high hopes for the night, that getting upset over such a small thing seemed completely short-sighted.

After they finished dinner and a few glasses of wine Paul slipped the door-man a few bills, which allowed them to see the real hidden gem of the restaurant, a tour of the elaborate wine cellar that the owners Jack Kriendler and Charlie Berns had installed in case of any government raids. In order to access the hidden spot someone had to insert a nearly-two-inch skewer into a specific crack in one of the brick walls, deactivating a lock, and allowing for the wall to be pushed back. Paul was truly impressed, and he thought it was no wonder it was never discovered during any prohibition raids. It also probably helped that, on top of everything else, the secret cellar actually ran under a neighboring restaurant, making it even harder to track down by authorities.

Valentina wasn't as impressed as Paul had hoped she'd be with the hidden spot, but he himself was absolutely floored at not only seeing not the incredible selection they had of rare and next to impossible to find wines (over 2,000 bottles) and spirits, but even more so was when he was shown all the bottles that lay forever waiting for owners who would never come. Those owners, who resided in the upper echelon of society, had passed before they had been able to drink up their reserved drink of choice, which now sat here, unclaimed and immortalized.

After the tour, they cabbed over to the Sutton Theater to see what would eventually end up being the biggest film of 1969 after it brought in a final U.S. gross of over a hundred million dollars. They both seemed to enjoy the film, with Paul being a real fan of westerns, and Valentina, like pretty much every other woman worldwide at that point, being a real fan of Paul Newman.

Their first official date would end how every time they got together ended, with the two of them ravishing each other's bodies, the world around them seemingly melting away during those moments that seemed like a different lifetime to Paul now. It was something Paul missed and longed for every time he saw Valentina even remotely nude these days, because even if they were to find their bodies intertwined with one another like the days and nights of the past, Paul knew in his heart of hearts that far too much had happened for either of them to ever be allowed to feel that naiveté ever again.

What a heartbreaking thought for anyone to carry around with them, but that is exactly what Paul lived with, each and every day—with each and every one of those days bleeding into each and every night.

———

Paul stood in a dimly lit, dingy, alleyway holding a Fie Arminius .357 Magnum in his outstretched arms as he listened to the street salesman's pitch.

"It's got a steel frame, double action, ventilated rib, with a large target grip. It's got the swing out cylinder, one stroke ejection, an internal hammer safety block, and an adjustable micro rear sight," the street salesman said, as Paul aimed it to and fro, one eye closed, trying to get a feel for the piece in his hands.

"That's eight," Paul said, still aiming the piece.

"What?"

Paul pulled the gun down to his side, turning to look at the street salesman, who had set up shop in the shadows of the seedy alleyway.

"You said you had ten reasons why I should own the Fie Arminius .357 Magnum, but you're two reasons short," Paul said, causing the street salesman to laugh.

"Shit, Byron said you were on a trip when he called about you needing a piece. This here gun have anything to do with whoever did that to your face?"

"Look, I'm not here shopping for a fucking conscience, man," Paul quipped, prompting the dealer to hold up his hands as a sign of peace.

"That's fair. You got me there. Reason number nine is the gun's untraceable, and reason ten... just shoot the fucking thing."

"What? Here? What about the cops?"

"You're in Harlem. Just another shot on a hot summer's day," the salesman replied, mere seconds before Paul abruptly pointed the gun directly at him! "What the hell, Jack?"

Paul knew the man was scared, and rightfully so, but Paul also knew this wasn't the first time he'd had a gun pointed at him. Something in the eyes gave it away, and it was something Paul had seen before in the eyes of others when he had pointed a gun at them. There was always a certain kind of calm. There was always a certain kind of acceptance. *It was something that was nearly impossible to describe to someone who had never seen it before*, Paul thought to himself, *but clearly...this man had it in his eyes*.

Paul thought about the Illinois boy, smiling and laughing as bullets continued to flying all around him, with half his fucking face missing, for the briefest of moments. He had had that look too, right before Paul pulled the trigger, putting him out of his misery.

BANG! BANG! BANG! BANG! BANG! BANG!

After a quick pivot, Paul fired the six shots, one after another, into a nearby brick wall.

"Okay. Okay. I see. Not your first time pulling a trigger," the salesman said, with one eye on Paul, the other still on the gun in Paul's hand.

"Special Forces. 1st Cavalry Division," Paul replied, his response allowing the salesman to calm down enough to make his way over to Paul, nodding his head. The mood and energy between them quickly shifted to one of mutual respect for a fellow brother-in-arms.

"Airborne Infantry. 11th Pathfinder Company."

"So, how much for the .357, soldier?" Paul asked.

"Book value for the chrome one is $135. I can get close to $200 for it, but for a brother... just give me an even hundred."

"Done," Paul said, tucking the piece into his waist, before peeling off five twenty-dollar bills from a roll. He handed them to the salesman, who started to say something once the bills hit his palm, but Paul's mind had already started to drift off somewhere else.

He walked away from the salesman whose words became muted as the outlines of an old memory started to take shape inside his muddled head. Slowly the outlines started to fill in, and the loose, jumbled, and disjointed pieces eventually gave way to the fully realized and very vivid memory of the first time Paul ever saw a gun.

It was back in 1956, and Paul was six years old. His parents had been split up for only a few months when Paul's father showed up at his grandmother's house one particularly hot and muggy afternoon. Paul, his younger brother, and their mother had moved out of New York when his parents decided they were better off apart than they were together. Like most kids, Paul thought he was responsible for his parents splitting up, but unlike most children, he was actually right—although in an indirect way.

A little over two years earlier, Paul started going to a daycare because both his parents worked, and there weren't any other family members to watch him during the day. As expected, Paul had a hard time adjusting to life away from his mother, but eventually he'd come around, and the daycare experience appeared uneventful. As is often the case, appearances can be misleading. Paul started wetting his bed at home and having nightmares, which led to long inquisitive conversations with his mom, who were rightfully concerned.

The actual details of what happened to Paul and eight other kids who attended the daycare thankfully became fragmented at best, but the damage was already done to both him and the entire family unit. It wouldn't be until years later, when the piece of shit that touched them was first eligible for parole that Paul sat down and really tried to revisit what had happened years earlier. He was in his early twenties by then, and the little trip down fucked-up memory lane was triggered by the retired prosecuting attorney actually calling him to tell him about the parole hearing. She thought a letter from the victims to the parole board might come into play on whether or not the pedophile was going to be released early, and although Paul would have been just fine never remembering any of what happened, he ultimately sat down and wrote the letter.

After Paul finally admitted to his probing mother what had happened to him, the police were called, and they, along with therapists and social workers, would ultimately reach out to interview the other children who attended the daycare. The results of the interviews were wild, with the children claiming they were raped with knives and other various items, even a magic wand. There was also talk of being touched by a clown in a magic room. Paul remembered being driven around in a car with his mother and two police detectives, looking for the building with the magic room. He wasn't entirely sure, but he didn't remember ever finding it, though. Some of the children told those interviewing them that they were forced to drink urine. Another said they were tied naked to a tree for hours. Paul didn't remember any of these particular things happening, at least not anymore, but he was sure that not remembering was probably for the best.

What he did remember were the steps that led up to the courthouse. He was looking at them in the distance as the prosecuting attorney was down on one knee talking to him before they entered the building. Paul remembered his mother was next to him, and that the attorney was telling him everything was going to be okay, and that all he had to do was to tell the truth. He also said that he was going to be in the courtroom, but that Paul didn't have to look at him if he didn't want to. The *"he"* that the attorney was referring to was the defendant—the man who had sexually abused him. Paul heard everything that was said, and he even responded to both the attorney and his mother when they asked him if he was okay, but the whole time his eyes were focused on those looming steps in the distance.

The actual trial, and Paul's participation in it, was little more than a blur. He remembered sitting in the witness chair. He remembered the judge talking to him. He remembered both the prosecuting attorney and the defense attorney asking him questions. He also remembered he was seated specifically so his back was to the defendant, so he didn't have to look at him. What Paul couldn't remember, though, was what any of those people looked or sounded like, and he certainly couldn't remember what he was asked, or how he had answered.

His time in that courtroom became a microcosm of his entire childhood. Everything was so fragmented. His entire childhood was now just a series of fragmented pieces of memories, including the years that would follow those days in that courtroom. Even when he tried, there would always be giant gaps, black space that should have held vivid memories of growing up. He should have been able to recall things in some kind of chronological order, but his mind didn't work that way, at least when it was trying to remember his days as a youth. Everything was jumbled on that timeline, just floating about without ties to place and time.

Paul tried to remember a time when his mom and dad were happy together, but the best he could muster was the time a bee stung his hand. Paul was sure that they all still lived together at the house where this happened, but he couldn't see the house itself. He did remember a frog that had hopped under a rock in the yard. When Paul reached his hand under the rock later that day, a bee stung him. The only other memories he could piece together from that place was when the family dog died he saw his father carrying its lifeless body out of the house with tears in his eyes. That was it, though. All Paul could muster was two memories from a place they must have lived at for years, with those years being ones after those days in the courthouse.

It was the middle of July when the three-month trial finally came to an end. The jury deliberations lasted twelve days, before they found him guilty on all indictments. He was sentenced to thirty to forty years in prison. The man who had molested him and eight other innocent kids was off to jail, while his victims were left to try to put together the pieces they were left with, in an effort to live as close to a normal life as possible as they moved forward.

For Paul, those pieces came with years of therapy, and those missing memories, both good and bad, that were locked away somewhere deep inside his subconscious. For some of the other children, those pieces ended up being far worse. Some of the victims would suffer from various mental health issues like chronic depression and eating disorders, with some of them even attempting suicide. Paul was also no stranger to attempting to take his own life, but his efforts to end things early failed. Tragically, two of the other victims succeeded. Years had passed since their innocence had been stolen, but both of them never made it past their teenage years.

The more immediate effects of being molested, at least in Paul's case, was the family falling apart, a little more each day, until Paul's mother and father finally called it quits. His father would go MIA for years, succumbing to his demons of being an alcoholic and even ending up homeless for a period of time. He wouldn't really come back into Paul's life again until he was a teenager, and despite his best efforts to make up for lost time, no one was getting those missing years back. Paul's mother would push through, sacrificing everything to raise her two boys for years, but eventually she too would crack. Paul was sure she was undiagnosed bipolar, and once he graduated from high school the two would become estranged from one another, off and on, for the rest of her life.

Paul's grandparents, his mother's parents, lived in Massachusetts, just outside of Cape Cod, and had welcomed them with open arms when they had shown up, seemingly out of nowhere one day. In hindsight, Paul was sure his grandparents had thoughts of "I told you so" running through their heads when it came to their daughter's choice of a spouse, but those thoughts never made it to their lips, at least not in front of Paul or his little brother, Gary, who had just turned three. No, all he or his brother ever saw out of his grandparents, from that day forward, was unconditional love and support. Even with their love, though, his childhood would be a few happy moments were speckled throughout a whole lot of darkness. The first time Paul ever saw a gun was certainly a part of that darkness.

His father's beloved Chevrolet Advance-Design truck was only a few years old when Paul saw it pulling up his grandparent's long and winding driveway. His father loved that truck from the day he bought it, until the day he finally had to put it to rest in a junkyard just outside of Buffalo, New York decades later, but he was hardly the only one. At the time, Chevrolet trucks dominated the competition, and were number one in sales in the United States for nearly a decade, from 1947-1955. All Paul really remembered about the truck itself was the cargo bed with the wood-plank floor, because it was where Paul—and the family dog—would often ride if they weren't going very far. That was, at least until the family dog was hit by a car and died.

Paul actually only rode in the truck a few times, before his parents called it quits, but each of those few times had made his mother nervous when he sat back in that cargo bed. Despite his mother's fears, though, Paul never fell out on any of those short trips.

On the day Paul saw his father's Chevy truck winding up the driveway, there was no one riding in the cargo bed, but it wasn't empty either.

His old man had been drinking. Paul knew it almost immediately when he stepped out of the truck, although his old man and drinking were hardly a rare sight. In fact, Paul was quite sure he got his penchant for being able to handle strong drink from his father. His old man had barely closed the driver's side door before he was reaching back into that cargo bed with the wood-plank floor, pulling up a hunting rifle. That was the first time Paul ever saw a gun.

Paul was sitting on the granite steps that led from the driveway up to the front door, watching as his father stumbled away from the truck, wielding the loaded rifle in his hand while shouting his ex-wife's first name at the top of his lungs. He looked like an insane person, with his face beet red with rage, his dark grey t-shirt soaked with sweat, as he continued to stumble about, his speech heavily slurred and his eyes glazed over. Paul tried to talk to his father, but he walked right past him, almost as if he didn't exist, on his way to the front porch of the house, still screaming at the top of his lungs the entire way. All that screaming would eventually get some attention inside the house, and Paul would forever remember the look on his grandmother's face as she came outside.

Paul's brother and grandfather had gone to the grocery store, and he was pretty sure that his mother was actually out on a date with another man, leaving him alone with only his grandmother during his father's impromptu visit. His grandmother was tough as nails, though, an immigrant who came over with her parents from the Greek island of Lesbos decades earlier, eventually starting her own family. Paul's mother was the oldest of seven children. Before she became a mother however, his grandmother was a nurse for the United States Army during World War I, actually working and living through live combat for nearly two years, from 1917-1919. So, this may have been Paul's first time seeing a gun, but it was far from the first time for his grandmother, and clearly it showed. She walked right up to his father, screaming back in his face, despite the loaded rifle in the much larger man's hands.

For some reason, Paul wasn't afraid for his grandmother. He wasn't even afraid for his own life. Paul remembered feeling two very clear and distinct feelings about the events that were unfolding in front of him, the first being anger toward his father for yelling at his grandmother, and the second was the one and only time he'd ever feel ashamed of his old man. Both of those feelings led to this not only being the first time Paul saw a gun, but also the first time he had one pointed at him, as he quickly ran in between the two screaming adults and shouted at his old man to leave his grandmother alone.

The Winchester Model 54 bolt-action rifle was the first to be mass produced for civilian use back in the 20's. One of over 50,000 that were made, this particular one was bought by his father's father and handed down to his son, who would eventually do the same when it was gifted to Paul years later. In this moment of his memory, though, the barrel of this particular rifle was pointed directly at Paul's forehead. He didn't flinch. He didn't have to, because something finally clicked on inside of Paul's father's head when he looked into his boy's eyes, and for the second and last time ever, Paul saw his old man cry.

The tears started to stream down his face. The gun was lowered and all the screaming stopped, then Paul and his grandmother watched his old man walk back down the granite stairs, back toward the truck he loved. They watched as he threw the rifle into the cargo bed with the wood-plank floor, and they watched him climb inside, before backing it down that long and winding driveway, as quickly as possible in his inebriated state. Then he was gone, and he and his grandmother would never talk about that day. All that was left was Paul's memory, his interpretation of the first time he ever saw a gun, the first time he had had a gun pointed at him, and the second time he would ever see his old man cry.

Now, the Winchester Model 54 bolt-action rifle was doing nothing more than collecting dust under Paul's bed inside his tiny New York apartment. Paul was quite certain he would never be pointing it at his daughter's forehead, but he could see himself continuing the tradition of passing it down, when the time was right. Assuming that he would be able to get out of this current mess alive so he would be able to do so.

Not long after buying the gun, Paul scurried into a phone booth on a street corner, closed the door, and frantically looked through what was left of the provided phonebook. "Come on. Belmore... Belmore."

He found the number he needed, dropped some change into the payphone, and quickly dialed. It started to ring. "Come on. Pick up," he said, but it just kept on ringing, until when he was about to hang up he heard a voice on the other end of the line.

"Hotel Belmore," the desk clerk said, as if he could care less about anything or everything.

"Can you connect me to room 202?"

"Just a minute," was followed by more ringing in Paul's ear.

"Answer the damn phone, Stephanie!" Paul cried out, as the ringing continued, but she never answered, sending him into a tailspin. "Fuck!" Paul slammed the phone down over and over again, before quickly exiting the booth and heading straight across the street to the subway station.

Paul sat in the all-too-familiar subway car, staring at the site from his fight with the hoods. Maybe it was because of budgetary reasons, or maybe it was because no one gave a fuck, but either way, the cracked windows had been poorly patched up as a temporary fix. A few patrons were scattered throughout. There was no sign of the hoodlum, as the train made a scheduled stop, a few of those patrons got off, and a few more got on. Still no hoodlum, though.

Paul stood up, the look of frustration on his face said it all, as the train continued on, and his time continued to...slip...away.

Paul paced back and forth, a lit cigarette hanging out of his mouth, his eyes nervously scanning his surroundings, and sure enough, the sky opened up and rain started to fall. Paul hesitated for a moment, before running across the street and into the unrelenting chaos between citizens and civil servants that made up the interior of the local police station.

Right in the middle of the worst retrenchment in NYPD history (from July 1975 until November 1979, no police officers were hired or trained in the city), the place was overwhelmed with foot traffic, but severely understaffed to accommodate it.

"Excuse me," Paul said as he approached the desk sergeant, who was more than underwater with numerous people all vying for his attention at the same time. "I need to speak to a detective."

"Fill it out, and wait for your name to be called," the desk sergeant replied, without even looking up, as he handed him a clipboard and the attached form.

"It's...it's important," Paul said, visibly flustered with being blown off.

"Yeah. They all are."

"But I need to confess to a crime."

"And we'll be with you shortly," the desk sergeant said dismissively, his eyes still down on the stacks and stacks of paperwork in front of him. Paul reluctantly took the clipboard, and turned to look at the countless number of people who were here before him, all waiting to be helped.

"It's about a murder," Paul muttered, finally causing the desk sergeant to look up. Paul finally had his attention.

Not long afterwards, Paul found himself sitting across from an overworked and overweight detective in his fifties. Wearing a tired suit, the man sat at his cluttered desk with a clipboard and a cup of coffee, looking completely annoyed with all of it.

"Okay, you wanted to confess a crime? I'm all ears," the detective said to Paul, who was distracted by the zoo of activity happening all around them. "Hey pal, you with me? I ain't got all day."

"Sorry. All of this is a...it's a bit overwhelming."

"Yeah? You should try working here. Now. This crime?"

"Right," Paul lit up a cigarette, before starting in with, "A few nights ago I –"

"Can you be more specific," the detective cut in, pen in hand, impatiently waiting to write.

"Right. It was a...it was Sunday."

"The 10th?"

"Right," Paul replied, as the detective started to write. "I...I witnessed a stabbing on the D train, and I never reported it."

"You witnessed a stabbing?" The detective said, as he abruptly stopped writing, putting down the clipboard and pen.

"Yes, sir."

"But you said you wanted to confess to a crime."

"Well, I didn't report it. Isn't that a crime?"

"In this city?" Now it was the detective's turn to light up a smoke. "Jesus, pal."

"I just want to help, because...because I should have tried to help then," Paul said, as the detective just eyed him for a beat, before finally relenting with a sigh.

"Okay. Did you know the victim?"

"No, sir. He was just some drunk."

"Shocking. How about the guy, the one doing the stabbing?"

"No, I...just some punk."

"Well, would you at least recognize him if you saw him again?" the detective asked, clearly agitated with their whole exchange at this point.

"Of course."

"Great. Then we'll start there," the detective said, opening up his desk drawers, and pulling out a stack of binders and sliding them across to Paul. "Go through these mugshots, and let me know if you see him."

"I will. Thank you," Paul said, as he started to flip through the pages of the first binder, slowly scanning the various faces on the page, before turning to the next.

"Look, pal, I got this psycho, this *Son of Sam* character, has the whole damn city scared, and it's almost been a month since the shootings in Bayside. This prick isn't going to stop until we get him, so if you don't mind I would really like to –"

"Of course. Say no more. I don't need you to hold my hand. Do what you have to do, detective."

The shooting he was talking about happened in Bayside, Queens less than a month earlier. Judy Placido and Sal Lupo had just left a disco and were sitting in Lupo's car when they were both shot. Paul saw in a column from Jimmy Breslin in the Daily News that both had survived their injuries, but still, the detective was more than right. This killer had everyone on edge, and for good reason. He had terrorized a whole city for a whole year by that point, and there would still be one more attack before he would finally be arrested.

The first victims attributed to him were shot and killed in the Bronx on July 29, 1776. In the Belham Bay area, two eighteen-year-olds, Jody Valenti and Donna Lauria, were sitting in Jody's parked Oldsmobile. Three bullets ripped through the car windows. One of them killed Donna instantly, the second left Jody with a bullet lodged in her thigh, and the third missed both of them. Jody would live to give a description of the perp, describing him as a white male in his thirties with short, dark, curly hair. She had his height at approximately 5' 8", and that he weighed in at around two hundred pounds. Her description ended up being pretty remarkable considering it would match the man who would eventually be arrested for the crimes to a tee.

Nearly three months after the first attack, the killer would strike again, shooting at Carl Denaro and Rosemary Keenan as they sat in a parked car in Flushing, Queens. This attack was in a residential area, with both victims surviving, but they were far from unscathed. Denaro was struck in the head with one of the bullets. He'd eventually need a metal plate to replace part of his skull. At the time, police had no idea the two attacks were connected, especially considering that they occurred in two different boroughs, which meant two different police precincts handled the cases.

A month had passed when sixteen-year-old Donna Demasi and her eighteen-year-old friend Joanne Lomino were walking home from a movie when they were approached by a man dressed in military fatigues. He shot each of them once before running away, leaving Demasi shot in the neck, and Lomino shot in the back. Demasi would make a full recovery, but Lomino wasn't as fortunate. She would end up being paralyzed from her injury.

The new year would start with another attack, as Christine Freund and her fiancé John Diel were shot in his car on January 30, 1977. After the initial shots were fired, Diel was able to speed away from the killer, most likely saving his life, but it was already too late for his love. Christine Freund would later die from her injuries at the hospital. The police would soon publicly acknowledge that there were similarities between this attack and earlier incidents, along with the fact that all of the victims had been shot with a .44 caliber bullet. The killer's weapon of choice brought with it the nickname the .44 Caliber Killer from the media. The name would stick until the killer eventually referred to himself as *The Son of Sam* in a handwritten letter found at a later crime scene and addressed to NYPD Captain Joseph Borrelli.

On the night of March 8, 1977, a Columbia University student who lived only a block away from the last attack was walking home from class when she was approached by a man with a gun. Despite her best efforts to shield herself with the textbook she was carrying, the bullet still managed to go through it cover to cover, penetrating her head. Virginia Voskerichian died before her body even hit the sidewalk.

The handwritten letter to Captain Borrelli was found on April 17, 1977, along with the bodies of Alexander Esau and his girlfriend Valentina Suriani. Both of them had been shot twice, with Esau already dead by the time the authorities arrived, and Suriani passing away later in the hospital. Along with referring to himself as *The Son of Sam*, the letter also promised that the killing would continue.

Initially the existence of the letter was kept from the public, but it would soon prove all for naught with the arrival of a second letter—this one sent directly to Daily News columnist, Jimmy Breslin. Breslin would initially send it to the police, but it would become public knowledge ten days later when the Daily News published a redacted version of the letter. The issue would be one of the biggest selling issues ever, topping more than one million copies sold.

The published piece, along with more information about the commonality of long dark hair among all of the targeted victims, would start a haircut and hair-dye frenzy across the women of New York City. With the police seemingly no closer to arresting a suspect, the impromptu haircut craze was just one result of the swelling fear that was running rampant and unchecked amongst New Yorkers at this point. People were terrified, and the pressure on the police was quickly mounting, as the public's fear was channeled into anger pointed directly toward the lack of results. The next attack on June 26th, the one the detective had mentioned to Paul, only added more fuel to that growing fire, but *The Son of Sam's* reign of terror was almost over.

Almost.

On July 31, 1977 Robert Violante and Stacy Moskowitz were out on a first date. Their date would end with Violante losing an eye and Moskowitz dying eighteen hours later. It would also end with a nearby eyewitness coming forward a few days later with information that would finally put an end to all of the madness.

The witness told the police they had seen a man they thought was holding a gun in a nearby Brooklyn neighborhood, only a few minutes before the Violante-Moskowitz shootings happened. The neighborhood just so happened to be one where parking tickets were being issued that night, with one of the tickets being given to a car that was registered to a man named David Berkowitz.

On August 10, 1977, police were staked outside Berkowitz's apartment. They waited until he got into his car and then arrested him. Inside the car they found maps of crime scenes and in a bag in the front seat was the infamous .44 caliber revolver. For Berkowitz, part of the thrill through the whole ordeal was the cat and mouse going on with the police department. But the game was finally over. The cat had won, and Berkowitz conceded as much as he sat behind the wheel of his car with a smile, telling the arresting officers, "Well, you got me."

He confessed to being *The Son of Sam*, and to the shootings, the next day. When detectives probed him on his motive, he simply said Sam had told him to do it. According to Berkowitz, the Sam in question happened to be his neighbor's black Labrador. It wasn't a surprise to anyone involved when he entered an insanity plea, but what it was when he changed his plea of guilty to six murders on May 8, 1978. He would receive six consecutive 25-years-to-life sentences.

"I hope you find *The Son of Sam* soon. And if I find the guy who did the stabbing in here, I'll be sure to let you know," Paul said, tapping the mugshot binder that lay open before him..

The detective nodded thankfully, got up from his desk, and left Paul alone to continue to peruse page after page of grim-looking criminals.

As soon as the detective was out of sight, Paul flipped frantically through the pages, scanning as quickly as he could. He found no luck in the first and moved quickly on to the second. Page after page, it was just more of the same: a motley crew of pimps, junkies, thieves, rapists, pedophiles, and murderers. They came from all walks of life, their ages spanning from late teens to geriatric, but none of that mattered between these yellowed and tattered pages. They were an obstinate bunch of repeat offenders, either too stupid, too broken, or too poor for any real chance at significant reform. If there was one physical commonality between them, it was something in the eyes, and that something seemed to fluctuate equally between evil and tragedy.

And then the face of the hoodlum was staring back at him. His mugshot was on the top of the second to last page in the second binder, third photo from the left, nestled between a youthful black boy who had an addiction to matches and gasoline, and a bearded white guy with ties to the Hell's Angels.

Paul looked up slowly, eyes darting around the room. Once he was sure that no one was looking, he clicked open the binder and removed the entire page. He tucked it inside his shirt and, with one last furtive glance around the room, fled the scene.

Not long after, Paul stepped into the upscale building's elevator, followed by the doorman who closed the door, turned the key, and pressed the PH button. Drenched from the rain, Paul watched the water continually drip from the front of his hair down onto the floor of the elevator as it slowly rattled upwards. The two men stood in silence for a moment, before the doorman finally spoke up.

"Carrying a little light there, aren't you?"

Paul just looked at him, completely perplexed with the question but not saying a word in response, which only seemed to agitate the massive man.

"He's expecting product, and he isn't a fan of surprises. He's not going to be happy."

"Yeah, well then, he can join the club. Do I look happy to you?" Paul asked.

"Do I look like I give a shit about your disposition?" The doorman's response brought with it some more awkward and uncomfortable silence between them again. "Tell me something, Whatta you weigh, buck eighty, buck eighty-five?"

"Something like that. Why?" Paul asked, as the doors finally opened on the top floor.

"Just preparing myself for how much extra dead weight I might be carrying in a few minutes is all," the doorman answered, as Paul went to step out of the elevator before his path was physically blocked.

"Hold up. You're not really going to insult me by making me frisk you are you?" Paul hesitated, not sure what to do. "Look, I've got plenty of my own. You make it out of there alive, and I promise I'll return it you ya. Deal?"

"Like I have an option," Paul replied, as he handed the doorman the gun from his waistband, prompting him to finally let him pass.

Once inside the penthouse suite, Paul was once again surrounded by those countless beauties in nothing but their bras and panties. Chevy was all smiles at the sight of Paul's entrance. "Paul, babydoll! So good to see you," he said, before turning to one of the girls, "Get him a towel."

He kissed Paul on both cheeks.

"Hey, Chevy. We need to talk," Paul said, causing Chevy to step back, staring at him but still wearing that smile, as one of the girls returned and handed Paul a towel to dry off. "Thank you for the towel."

"Okay, let's grab a drink then. Come on," Chevy replied, as he started to walk toward the other room.

"I don't have time for a drink. I need your help," Paul said, his words finally making the smile fade from Chevy's face.

"Well, that's obvious, dear, with you coming here empty-handed and knowing I'm waiting on product. Now. Let's go."

Paul reluctantly followed him into the bar area, where the bartender quickly set up two glasses. "What are ya drinking?"

"Beer's fine."

Chevy took a seat, and playfully patted the seat next to him for Paul to sit as he placed his order with the waiting bartender. "Two whiskeys neat," he said, as Paul sat down. "It may be pouring outside, but '*Whiskey is liquid sunshine.*'"

"Who was that? Bernard Shaw?"

"Yes. You know, you never cease to impress me, which is why you coming here empty-handed is such a...surprise."

"Look, Chevy, I mean no disrespect, and –"

Chevy held up his hand for Paul to stop, as the bartender poured the whiskey, barely finishing before Chevy pounded his and then stared at Paul until he reluctantly did the same. "Good, boy. Okay, you have my undivided attention. What pains your beautiful little heart?"

"I have to find this guy," Paul replied, sliding the page of mugshots over to Chevy and pointing at the hoodlum's picture.

"And what's this have to do with my business?"

"You really want to know?"

Chevy thought about it for a moment before turning his attention to the bartender. "We'll take another round."

"Chevy, please, no more drinks, I just want –"

Chevy abruptly slammed his knife into the bar, quickly cutting off Paul's plea. "So let me guess, this guy is the reason I'm going to look like a fool to my friends when I can't deliver what I promised?"

"Look, this wasn't supposed to happen like this," Paul answered, just as two more drinks were placed in front of them and both were quickly downed in unison.

"So...why did it then?" Chevy said, as he looked over Paul's shoulder, prompting Paul to follow his eyes to reveal the doorman dressed in a rain-coat and carrying a large, rolled up, plastic drop-cloth and standing in the doorway.

"You don't have to do this," Paul pleaded.

"You're giving me advice on how to run my business now, Paul?"

The doorman started to make his way over to them, as Chevy pulled the knife out of the bar, and pointed it at Paul.

"No. Of course not."

"Another round, please," Chevy said to the bartender. The doorman was now standing directly behind Paul, prompting him to actively start eyeing his surroundings, looking for any way out of this mess. "Good, because I hope you will believe me..." Chevy continued, just as the bartender started to pour the next round, but the man never got to finish the task. "...when I tell you that I know what I'm doing!" Chevy finished speaking, mere seconds before he abruptly plunged the knife into the bartender's throat!

"Shit! What the fuck?!" Paul gasped, as the bartender tried to struggle. Chevy made it a point, though, to use his other hand to pull the man's head down, while he continued to dig the knife further into his throat, turning it the whole time for some added emphasis.

"You thought you could steal from me, you piece of shit?!" Chevy asked his doomed employee. The bartender was obviously dead at this point, but Chevy continued to grind the knife into his throat, as blood started to pool all over the bar.

Finally, he pulled the knife out, and motioned for the doorman, who in turn started to clean up the mess, as he asked, "And will I be carrying any extra weight outta here this evening, sir?" They were both looking at Paul, who did his best to hide his growing fear.

"No, that'll be it for tonight. Killing you, Paul, would be a piss poor business decision," Chevy said. The doorman nodded, as he unrolled the plastic drop cloth and took to wrapping up the body in it before dragging it away, allowing Chevy to once again return his attention to the mugshot in front of him. "So, this is all ya got?" He asked, as he picked it back up again, using a bar rag to wipe away some blood. "A picture?"

"Afraid so," Paul responded, noticeably distracted by the blood on the bar counter, prompting Chevy to snap his fingers in his face.

"Are you still with me, Paul?"

"Yes. Sorry. So, can you help? I...I don't have a lot of time."

"I help you find this guy, and we're back on schedule?" Chevy asked. Paul nodded his head "yes." "Then yes. Give me a few hours."

"Thank you, Chevy."

"Don't thank me yet. How can I reach you when I find him?"

"Hotel Belmore. Room 202," Paul replied, his words instantly souring Chevy's face.

"Jesus, you're really slumming it. If I knew you were staying in that shithole, I wouldn't have let you in tonight."

Paul got up, but Chevy quickly lunged over and grabbed him by the hand. "Aren't you forgetting something?" Paul just looked at him, no answer for the question, until Chevy finished pouring their third round and handed the glass to Paul.

"Right. Cheers."

"To making things right," Chevy said, as they clinked their glasses and drank.

"I also meant to ask you if you've seen Stephanie tonight."

"No. She's probably dancing at that disgusting bookstore."

"Yeah. You're probably right. Thanks," Paul said, as he once again tried to leave.

"Hey Paul, give it to me straight, just tell me..." Chevy called out, causing Paul to stop and turn back around, "...is our girl okay?"

Paul hesitated for a moment, before, "I...I hope so." They shared a look, ending with Chevy eventually nodding his understanding before he turned and poured himself another drink as Paul finally left the room.

Despite the rain continuously falling outside, business in the adult bookstore didn't seem to be suffering much as Paul made his way past the numerous patrons on his way to the counter.

"Is she here?" he asked the foxy teller, who was all smiles as she looked him up and down, her entire being dripping with sexual intentions. She was practically purring as she seductively bit her lower lip before finally answering.

"I'm right here, baby?"

"Stephanie. Is she working?" The teller actually looked disappointed as she put her head down to read a magazine.

"Like I know any of their names. Knock yourself out," she said, gesturing toward the back. Paul blew by her on his way back to the booths. The teller stared at his ass as he left. "What a waste," she said to herself. As soon as he was out of sight completely she called out, "Hey Byron!"

Moments later, Paul dropped a quarter into the slot, and nervously started to pace back and forth, his boots sticking to the ground with each step as he impatiently waited. Slowly the dark window in front of him started to go up.

"Come on!" he cried out.

Inch by inch the barricade gave way to the sheet of plexiglass that had been dulled with those various scratches and graffiti.

"Stephanie..."

Legs. Long, seductive, legs were the first bit of flesh before his eyes, prompting him to bang on the plexiglass, as the partition continued to rise. "Hey!" he screamed, as he continued to bang, trying to get the attention of the scantily clad seductress on the side, who was...not Stephanie. "Shit!"

The other dancer, a beauty in her own right but far from being his dancer, pointed to her ears, and mouth. "What's wrong?"

Paul didn't even bother responding, choosing to just sit back on the seat instead. He was lost, somewhere between relieved and annoyed, as the partition eventually started to go back down. The other dancer knocked on the glass, trying to get his attention, but Paul was already heading for the door.

He opened it up, and found himself staring directly at Byron.

"Where's my girl at, square?" Bryon asked, a loaded gun pointed directly at Paul.

"I was hoping you could tell me," Paul replied, holding his hands up as Byron pushed the barrel of the gun into Paul's forehead, forcing him back into the booth in the process.

"Wouldn't know," Byron said, as he closed the door behind them. He reached into the waistband of Paul's pants, pulled out Paul's gun, and tucked it in his own. "You see, since you started comin' round, been seeing less and less of that fine ass."

"Look, I just came here because I was looking for her," Paul said, the gun still pressed firmly against his head.

"For her? And what's wrong with the bitch on the other side of that glass?" Byron asked, as he pushed the barrel of the gun harder into Paul's forehead. "Put a quarter in the slot."

"I don't have time for this."

"And I got bills to pay, and you comin' round here is fuckin with my stable. Not going to tell you again. Put a fuckin' quarter in the slot!"

"Okay, okay. Going to reach into my pants pocket," Paul said.

"Slowly."

Paul reached into his pocket, and pulled out a quarter. "Stephanie told me you've been taking care of her since she was young."

"Yeah, that's right. That bitch owes me," Byron said, as Paul slowly moved to the slot with the quarter, the barrel of the gun now aimed at the back of his head.

"You going to shoot me in the back?"

"Then how would I claim self-defense? Don't know if you noticed the color of my skin, but I gotta be extra careful with shit like this."

"And you need a witness," Paul said, putting it all together now.

"Yeah, that's right. A white bitch. To back up this black face. Ya dig?" Bryon said, as Paul dangled the quarter by the slot without depositing it.

"Put it in."

"No. You want your witness, you do it," Paul said, before dropping the quarter on the ground, and causing Byron to come screaming toward him with the gun leading the way.

"You think this is some kind of –?" Byron didn't get to finish, as Paul quickly dodged to the side, before delivering a quick open-hand to Byron's throat, sending the man spinning and the bullet firing harmlessly into the wall.

"She was just a kid!" Paul screamed.

There was nothing beautiful or graceful about what happened next. This wasn't some masterfully choreographed fight scene. This. Was. Pure. Ugly. Violence. Paul brought his elbow down across Byron's, knocking the gun to the ground, and breaking Byron's arm in the process. Byron dropped to the ground in agony, giving Paul the opening to reclaim the gun, tucking it back in his waistband, before he kicked Byron's away from him. Byron tried to scream, but he had no voice courtesy of Paul's first blow.

Noticeably struggling to breath, but not ready to give up, Byron started to crawl toward the dropped quarter. His fingers were mere inches away from grabbing it. "You piece of shit!" Paul screamed, as he kicked him right in the nuts, ending his pursuit of the loose change, and causing him to roll up in the fetal position. Paul went to continue his offensive attack, but stopped when he noticed his stitched knife-wound had started to bleed through his shirt.

"Shit!" Paul lifted up his shirt to reveal the stitches were indeed torn. "Damn it," he said as he put his shirt back down, and started toward Byron again, but apparently he wasn't the only one who noticed the open wound.

Using every ounce of remaining energy he had, Byron kicked right at the blood-spot on Paul's shirt, sending him backwards in obvious pain. With Paul momentarily reeling, Byron started to once again scramble for the quarter. "Help me! Someone...help!" Byron said. The words were barely audible, though, as Paul grabbed him by the leg. Byron managed to kick him off with the other foot, before scooping up the quarter, and depositing it in the slot.

As the divider started to slowly rise, Paul lunged forward, attaching his open hand to Byron's face, his fingers digging into Byron's eye sockets. Byron desperately tried to fight back, his one good arm flailing about, but it was a lost cause from the get-go.

"She was just a kid!" Paul cried out again, ramming every word home as forcefully as he dug his bloodied fingers deeper into the man's eye sockets. The divide had gotten high enough so that they could see those legs on the other side. Paul knew he was running out of time, but the ticking clock, and his desperation, only seemed to fuel his rage even more, as tears streamed down his face.

"She was..."

Blood poured from Byron's eye-sockets, as Paul, his fingers still firmly attached to what was left of Byron's eyes, started slamming him up against the wall, over and...over...and over...and over again, "...just a kid."

The divide had now risen high enough to see her belly-button, just as Byron went limp. Paul retracted his fingers from the bloody sockets, and was out the door before Byron's body even hit the floor.

With hysterical screaming coming from the back room, Paul made his way quickly through the main area of the store. All of the customers were so preoccupied with their own vices they didn't even notice Paul was covered from head-to-toe in Byron's blood, as he moved toward the exit. He reached the door, and was about to exit, when the teller called out to him. "Hey! Wait!"

Paul slowly turned around to see the teller was staring right at him. They locked eyes for a moment, leaving Paul unsure of what he should do next, until she gave him the answer with tears in her eyes. "Thank you."

Relieved, Paul nodded his head and quickly fled the place.

Paul made his way down the rain-soaked sidewalks, as a flash of lightning ripped through the summer sky. The rain, still pouring down from above, managed to wash away all the blood from his skin, hair, and clothing, but it did little to wash away the horrors of what he had experienced... of what he had inflicted.

Maybe we're all lost, and...

Moving with a purpose, he quickly made his way past the few souls who were also out braving the elements.

...constantly looking for something.

Some of them, like the junkies, were unable to take a day off from their vices. Others, like the pimps, prostitutes, and police stayed diligent to their chosen professions in any weather. Lastly, there were those who had no choice, no place to call home, and those poor souls were just doing their best to stay dry in any way possible.

Even if we don't know what it is we're all looking for...

The one thing that each of those groups had in common was that none of them noticed Paul. He certainly noticed them, though, especially the handful of police officers, who he did his best to avoid at all costs, for obvious reasons.

Yeah, maybe this whole fucking city was already lost.

Paul scurried into the subway terminal, just as another bolt of lightning engulfed the sky, followed by a monstrous rumbling of thunder.

Paul made his way inside the black and orange lobby of the Hotel Belmore, dripping water still falling off of him and on to the soiled and stained green carpet.

During the day, the Belmore's permanent residents, the old and tragically forgotten, mingle about the lobby, but once the sun sets...

Shivering, he quickly moved past the various malcontents, mostly under-aged prostitutes and their pimps, that populated the tattered furnishing.

...a different lost, and forgotten crowd takes over, because at seven dollars for four hours or ten for all night, the spot makes for a

convenient place for girls to take their Johns. Guessing Stephanie knew to take me here from her time turning tricks when she first arrived in the city.

5

Wednesday July 13th, 1977 at 8:37 PM

STREAKS OF LIGHTNING FLASHED ACROSS gloomy skies, before striking the Buchanan South electrical substation on the Hudson River and immediately tripping two circuit breakers.

Paul, now in dry clothes, finished redressing his wound, before he sat on the bed with his notebook in hand, writing down more of his endless stream of consciousness.

> *Like Stephanie, thousands of kids run away to New York City every year looking for something, and most of them just end up lost, because this city is no mother. And this city will weed out the weak, and spit them out.*

He stopped writing to look at the phone that refused to ring with some much-needed news from Chevy, before returning to his notebook.

> *And in the end, Stephanie was no different. I don't know why she did it. She seemed happy. Maybe that was just a front, though. A mask. Or maybe I'm to blame. Maybe what I said awakened those old demons. Or maybe the demons were never really asleep.*

Paul stopped writing, and turned to the other side of the bed to reveal why Stephanie never answered his frantic call from the phone booth. She never answered because she couldn't. The tourniquet was still wrapped tightly around her arm, the needle still stuck in her vein, and fresh white foam was still around her mouth.

Because you can't outrun your demons. Stephanie obviously tried. Who knows, maybe now her demons will finally let her rest.

Paul gently removed the tourniquet and needle, before wiping her mouth, and closing her eyelids. He pulled back the covers of the bed, and tucked her in, before kissing her forehead as if she were merely going to sleep for the night.

A true rest.

Stephanie Lynn Wheeler was in fact from Minnesota—Saint Paul to be exact. Saint Paul was at one point the home of Charles M. Schulz, F. Scott Fitzgerald, and August Wilson, who moved there in 1978. Wilson would end up premiering most of the ten plays in his Pittsburg Cycle at the Penumbra Theater, an African-American theater in Saint Paul that was founded by Lou Bellamy in 1976.

Saint Paul was also home to James Haakenson before he, just like Stephanie, became one of the 400 juvenile runaways that left Minnesota each year. Authorities believed James was killed in August in 1976, after his remains were found in 1978 in a crawl space under a home in the Chicago area along with more than two dozen other victims of serial killer John Wayne Gacy. He was one of eight who were buried without any form of identification. It wouldn't be until 2011, when the remains were exhumed in order to use DNA testing, that James Haakenson would be identified.

There are endless reasons why juvenile runaways leave home, but more times than not, they all share a commonality in having the final chapter of their lives end in some form of tragedy. James Haakenson, the twelve-year-old outside the Markwell Hotel, and now Stephanie were just three examples of those tragic stories. For Stephanie at least, her early childhood chapters were actually the farthest thing from tragic, a least until her older brother's death.

Stephanie was the youngest of two children who grew up in an upper middle-class home in a household that would be the envy of almost any child. Her parents were not only still together, but they were still in love, and their love carried over to Stephanie and Craig, who in turn were inseparable growing up, despite her brother being four years older. It was a strong family unity, one that offered the kind of support, compassion, and patience that almost seemed too good to be true to anyone on the outside looking in on them. But all of it was authentic. It was as close to perfect as a family could be, and perhaps it was that perfection when things were going right that caused things to fall apart when Craig got sick.

Stephanie was thirteen when the family got the news. It was the tail end of summer, and soon she and her girlfriends would have to go back to paying for their meals when they went to McDonald's because Craig would no longer work there once school was back in session. It didn't matter how long he had been gone for, because she could always close her eyes at any point and see his infectious smile as he handed them a bag that was practically overflowing even though they had only paid for a few apple pies. She knew he loved her, and enjoyed spoiling her and her friends, but she also was sure he got a real kick out of doing something that was wrong. It was on one of his shifts that he had gone completely white, before passing out completely and cracking his head on the permanently grease-ladened tile. Stephanie's dad picked her up from her best friend's house a few hours later, and the two of them drove in complete silence on their way to join her mother, who was already at the hospital waiting for Craig to wake up. That drive without words was the first sign that Stephanie's perfect childhood was about to take a drastic and permanent nosedive toward troubled waters, and everything that followed showed that none of them had even the slightest idea on how to navigate those waters.

Craig woke up not long after they arrived, and despite the fact that they were all gathered in a hospital room, he was his usual happy-go-lucky self almost immediately. It wasn't until years later Stephanie was able to take a step back from it all, replaying that day's events in her head, finally realizing that he was actually scared shitless, but he had no intention of showing it to anyone, especially not to his little sister. And that was Craig in a nutshell. He would rather strap on his trademark smile, and laugh until he was blue in the face to make sure his little sister and parents wouldn't suffer any more than he could see they already were, than to admit that he was scared and needed them to be the strong ones instead.

The doctors couldn't figure out why he had passed out, so they ran every test imaginable even though Craig swore to them he was fine, and all he wanted to do was to go home. When the doctors viewed his MRI they saw ring-enhancing lesions, which then required a stereotactic biopsy for pathologic confirmation. Craig just wanted out of that hospital bed. He wanted things to go back to the way they were before he had taken his fall. They all did, but when there's an inoperable brain tumor, at the end of the day it doesn't matter what anyone really wants, because the clock immediately starts ticking.

The doctors said the technical term for what Craig had was glioblastoma, an aggressive form of cancer that starts out in the cells that support a person's nerve cells. The doctors didn't think the tumor was operable, and gave him twelve to fifteen months to live. He didn't even last the twelve months, but it wasn't for a lack of trying.

The wheels didn't just come off for the entire family at that point, the whole fucking thing crashed and went up into flames, especially for Stephanie's mom and dad, who took the diagnosis as well as one might expect. Stephanie was too young to really grasp the specific details of what was going on, and all the medical terminology seemed to do was to confuse and scare her even more than she already was, but of course Craig just took it in stride, because that was Craig. He was seventeen going on no tomorrow, but yet he somehow managed to hold it together for the sake of all of them, while the rest of the family went sideways in their own unique ways.

The first few months Stephanie watched as her brother continued onward as if nothing had even happened, even starting his junior year of high school like the rest of his friends. Stephanie went back to school too, but really only in body, as her mind had floated off somewhere else almost immediately. It all felt surreal, like it was happening to someone else, because how could a thirteen-year-old girl truly grasp losing her brother in a year or so.

Checking out mentally, floating through life in a constant daydream of sorts, never really awake but never really asleep either, was a coping tactic Stephanie shared with her mother. They both were there physically, and they both continued about with their daily routines, but they were merely going through the motions on autopilot.

Stephanie's father came from a long line of drinkers, so he had been determined to break the cycle once Craig was born. He had been clean and sober since the day her brother was born, but after the diagnosis the operable word in that statement quickly became "was." After that point, Stephanie couldn't remember a time when he wasn't either passed out, drunk, or on his way to being drunk so that he could eventually pass out. She also got a good look on why he had been so adamant on breaking the cycle in the first place, but her vantage point was nothing compared to the firsthand look her mother got. Sober the man was a sweetheart, drunk he liked to use her mother as a punching bag. The actual details were far messier, so as far as Stephanie was concerned, the punching bag metaphor was more than enough to describe the situation.

Stephanie started skipping school. Then she stopped going all together. After three months, Craig had trouble even getting out of bed in the morning.

As the days and weeks went by, Stephanie saw less and less of him, as she did the rest of the family, because she just stopped coming home. No one seemed to notice, not even Craig, but at least he had the excuse of being hopped on all kinds of medications. And, of course, he was dying.

At first she would stay with friends, hopping from couch to couch whenever her friend's parents would start to complain about her being around so much. Eventually she started staying less and less with girlfriends, and more and more with boys, until she finally reached the point where she just wanted to get the hell out of Saint Paul all together.

Stephanie left just as skyscrapers and civic and environmental activism were all on the rise throughout Saint Paul. She left just moments after her brother took his last breath, while he was surrounded by the rest of the family, with each of them wearing their new identities while they said their goodbyes to the unconscious boy who had always been the glue that held them together. Dad was drunk. Mom was numb with absolute denial, and Stephanie's bags were already packed and waiting out in the hall. Along with her bags was a one-way bus ticket to New York City, with Byron waiting in the wings and constantly looking for new girls to add to his ever growing stable. Of course, meeting Byron was still a ways away, and it wouldn't happen until she hit rock bottom, but that's usually how those kinds of meetings happen.

There was little in the way of hyperbole when Stephanie said she was a kid who was a junkie, and that Byron ultimately saved her when she was a mess with a needle constantly in her arm.. She had barely left the Port Authority Bus Terminal at 8th Avenue and 41st Street, before the first of those needles were in her arm.

She had made arrangements to crash with a guy named Lawrence, who knew her brother from playing sports together, although he was a few years older than Craig. Lawrence had moved out to New York immediately after he graduated, chasing the acting bug, but ultimately ending up chasing the dragon instead, before eventually graduating to shooting junk. It took Stephanie all of two minutes to realize she had made a huge mistake with the temporary living situation. Lawrence never met her at the bus station like they had agreed, and when she was finally able to find her way to his place in the South Bronx, she had to step over a handful of other junkies who were crashing in the place just to find him passed out with his own needle still sticking out of his arm.

She was just thirteen years old, out of her hometown of Saint Paul for the first time in her life, living in a place not much larger than a walk-in-closet, surrounded by junk and junkies. In hindsight, she should have turned around right then and there. She should have made her way back to the bus terminal and caught the first bus back home. But she didn't, because in a lot of ways this situation was somehow less painful than the one she was running away from back in Minnesota. In this place, at least, she never had to helplessly watch what her parents had become since Craig had gotten sick. In this place, at least, she didn't have to pass by Craig's empty and cold bedroom that once was so warm and alive. In this place, she too could develop a habit, one that was all consuming, and one that would at least momentarily calm all the nightmares and heartbreaking memories that were otherwise on permanent rotation inside of her head.

No one ever pressured her to shoot junk, but that's the thing about junk. No one ever really has to pressure anyone to do it, particularly not a young teen who was struggling with real loss and abandonment. Stephanie started smoking it the same night she arrived at Lawrence's place. She would be shooting it a few days later, and the first time she did, that initial intravenous high hit her while she was still a virgin, but when she finally came to on the other side that would no longer be the case. Of course, everything was a blur, but she was sure it was Lawrence. What she couldn't be sure of, though, was whether or not it was just Lawrence.

So, as she developed a full-blown habit, it became more and more painfully clear that Lawrence hadn't invited her to crash out of the kindness of his heart, and as that habit took a real firm hold on her, that's when the real pressure began.

Turns out that being an aspiring actor doesn't exactly pay the bills, so Lawrence was always short on money for rent, and of course for junk, with the only commodity he had to barter with being one recent juvenile transplant from his hometown, who was conveniently junk dependent and just as desperate as he was for the next score. Days melted into weeks, weeks melted into months, and soon Stephanie had completely lost track of the highs, the lows, and even the turnstile of Johns that she was passed around to on the regular at that point. But even then, she still hadn't officially hit rock bottom, and she was still a ways away from meeting Byron.

It was sometime during late winter when mounting unpaid utility bills finally led to both the heat and electricity being turned off in the apartment, but theirs was far from the only one to see this outcome. The whole building was a reflection of junk life, the various units in varying degrees of decay like the endless track-marks across an addict's body, just dying for the next fix, but sitting in the cold and dark while waiting for a pusher who's never on time.

The junky highs off of doctor-prescribed drugs had been replaced with the surging heroin epidemic, and in 1971 more adolescents died from heroin overdoses than from any other cause, but because the majority of the deaths were centralized in lower class inner-city neighborhoods, there was little compassion both locally and nationally. Hell, there was barely any sympathy from within the actual junky community for that matter.

Stephanie's rock bottom started with a bad batch that made the rounds. By the time she noticed Lawrence's lips and fingernails had gone blue and that he was having trouble breathing, it was too little too late. The blood had already spurted into the dropper, and she had released the homemade tourniquet around her arm, causing the junk to empty into her vein. She knew something was wrong immediately, and in seconds she was completely disoriented. The last thing she remembered before waking up on a hospital bed was Lawrence's eyes, pleading to her for help that she was in no position to give him. Lawrence was pronounced dead on arrival the moment the paramedics wheeled him through the emergency room doors at Lincoln Hospital.

This was 1971, and in some respects, dying before you made it into Lincoln Hospital could be considered a blessing in disguise. One of the largest hospitals in the area, things were so bad there that the community actually took over the place just a year earlier in an attempt to fix the health issues in the Bronx, and the endless inadequacies of the hospital. One of those inadequacies was that the hospital was full of lead, and on many occasions, children would actually get lead poison when admitted to the Lincoln for other health issues.

Of course, none of this matters to a junky at any point while they were still using, and it especially didn't matter to one who had just overdosed, even after she came to and was admitted for observation and a detox. It was Stephanie's first and only detox, and at various points throughout it, she found herself wishing she had actually died on arrival like Lawrence.

When she left the hospital she actually managed to stay off of street junk for good, but one would be hard-pressed to consider the days and nights that made up her new found sobriety anything close to resembling clean. Over the days and weeks that followed, all she really did was swap her full-time drug habit with what was once only a part-time habit of turning tricks out of necessity but now became a full-time occupation.

At first, she worked any and all areas, whatever was closest to whatever couch she was able to crash on the night before, but it only took a few weeks of those freedoms for her to learn the hard way that there was no such thing as being a freelance prostitute. It only took a few nights for her to end up on the wrong street corner, at the wrong time, cornered by a pimp who didn't exactly see eye-to-eye with her entrepreneurial spirit.

She tried to chalk it all up to just being young and ignorant, but the pimp that set her straight wasn't exactly keen on listening to reason. He wasn't exactly keen on her even speaking really, as he pummeled her relentlessly with fists that were accented with heavy rings on more than a few fingers. The first punch hit her right in the middle of her chest, knocking the wind out of her and tearing her intercostal muscles, while also spraining the cartilaginous joints between her ribs and sternum. While she was keeled over, gasping for air that didn't seem to want to come, the second punch caught her directly in the mouth, knocking out almost all of her top teeth and fracturing her jaw. More punches followed, but mercifully, she was no longer awake to feel or remember them.

Her second stint in the luxurious Lincoln hospital was just as glamorous as the first, only this time the drugs making her high were prescribed and administered by the doctors and staff. Her street habit was at least momentarily replaced by Vicodin and Oxycodone, while she recovered from a beating that, the doctors were kind enough to remind her on more than one occasion, should have probably landed her in the morgue instead of in a hospital bed.

As fate would have it, though, she did survive the beating, but she was far from being in the clear. Six daunting months of physical rehabilitation became her newest hobby. It was a hobby that was almost constantly done while high, and one that had her eating and drinking out of a straw until her jaw healed. Then she was fitted for dental veneers to replace the row of missing top teeth in her mouth. It was somewhere in the middle of those daunting six months that Stephanie met Byron.

He came to see her when her mouth was still wired shut, her face puffy and swollen, and one of her eyes gruesomely bloodshot from a partially detached retina. She looked more like a broken fighter than anyone someone would pay money to sleep with, but Byron was always an opportunist who valued potential down the road and believed in buying low and selling high. He spent more than a few days and nights visiting with girls just like Stephanie, in each case using their unfortunate predicament to sell his services for security to make sure whoever put them in the hospital bed wouldn't return to finish the job. He invested in them when they were at their worst, playing the long game, finding and preying on potential new clients who were in recent medical distress, much like an ambulance-chasing attorney.

But Stephanie appreciated Byron coming to visit, and quickly took him up on his offer for both his immediate protection, as well as safe and profitable employment down the road. After all, she was well aware that no one else was coming to visit, but that offer came with a few stipulations.

Stephanie had become so emotionally and spiritually detached from sex by this point that the first stipulation, the one that called for her to forever be at his beck and call sexually, was never much of an issue. Byron was really no different than any of the endless Johns over her lifetime when it came to her giving herself up physically. The physical element was always little more than erotic performance art to her, and the ability for detachment allowed her mind and soul to wander elsewhere during each exchange.

She actually marveled, from time to time, at exactly where her mind and soul were able to wander to, the erotic physicality of the moment replaced with various exotic locales insider her head. The grunts and groans were replaced by the sound of waves lapping on the sandy beaches of California. The smells of oil, body odor, and sex were replaced by the smells of sunscreen and of the ocean. The feel of sweat and sperm on her skin was replaced with the feel of the sun and the cold Pacific Ocean on her body.

She saw the endless coastlines of Northern and Southern California, and wore luxurious clothes while she rubbed elbows with celebrities in the Hollywood hills. She saw the beauty of the islands of Greece and the endless history of the country's mainland. She walked amongst the ruins of gods in Rome, and drank incredible wine while she traveled the countryside in the South of France. She carried a designer umbrella in the rain while touring the streets and sights of London, before riding carefree on the back of a donkey as it made its way to the pyramids in Cairo.

In the end, her mind and spirit managed to travel all over the world, embarking on countless trips that made up a lifetime full of the most wondrous of experiences, all while her feet never actually touched land that wasn't outside of Minnesota or New York City. Byron also upheld his side of the bargain, keeping her safe while she turned tricks for him, and eventually keeping her under his roof when she transitioned off the street to dance at the bookstore. And, in the end, Stephanie didn't pick up another needle until the one that ultimately took her life that night at the Hotel Belmore.

Paul slowly walked to the window, pulling back the disgusting curtain to reveal the storm still raging outside, its fury only matched by the one that was forever building in his insides. A flash of lightning overwhelmed the sky for a moment, followed by the power going out, leaving Paul in the dark.

I know enough now not to run from my demons. So, I'm going to continue using them instead. At least until all of this is over.

He looked out the window. It was not just the hotel. He was not the only one in darkness.

Tonight the entire world would see what happens when a whole city was wound too tight for far too long.

The phone finally rang.

6

Wednesday July 13th, 1977 at 9:36 PM

THE ENTIRE CITY WAS SHROUDED in complete and total darkness. Neighborhood after neighborhood had gone completely dark...one...after...another. Even Shea Stadium was affected, losing power in the bottom of the sixth inning, with Lenny Randle at bat and the New York Mets losing 2–1 against the Chicago Cubs.

Chaos quickly escalated across the various New York City streets, as a Molotov cocktail sailed through the air before breaking through a storefront's glass window. Flames quickly overtook the window, with the rest of the store eventually following suit.

This was just the beginning.

> *Tonight the whole world would see that the people of New York*
> *City were tired of being lost. That they were tired of being forgotten.*

The New York City Blackout of 1977 would quickly take a stranglehold over the city. From Brooklyn to the Bronx, and everywhere in between... looting...arson...and violence erupted.

> *Tired of keeping their demons at bay, so instead...*

A dozen shirtless teens threw a brick through another window, before they kicked the remainder of the glass away, and climbed inside to go "shopping."

...they let them come out to play for the night.

Spliced starter-wires were put together, causing an engine to roar to life, just moments before a brand-new car was driven off the dealership lot, and it was far from the only one. One by one engines and headlights came on, before the boosted cars all drove away into the endless darkness.

Tonight, the inevitable was happening, and it was happening all around me.

More than a thousand fires were set that night and entire blocks were burned to the ground. When it was finally over, the looting and vandalism ended up hitting thirty-one neighborhoods. More than fifteen hundred stores were damaged. People flooded the streets, arms filled with various spoils from televisions to food and everything in between. But not every store owner was going down without a fight.

In one of those thirty-one neighborhoods, the barrel of a shotgun was placed right in a looter's face, prompting him to wisely put down what he was trying to steal and to back out of the store. Another store owner chased away potential looters with a large machete outside a different store, only a few blocks away from the first one. The store owners weren't the only ones looking out for the mom-and-pop stores in their neighborhoods, though. A group of locals, armed mostly with baseball bats, stood guard outside the grocery store that had helped feed generations in the area for decades.

Vastly outnumbered, the police battled with looters, with mixed results of both blood and handcuffs. More than five hundred police officers were injured, and more than three thousand looters were ultimately arrested.

I may have been constantly looking for something my whole life, but for once, at least at this exact moment, I knew exactly what I was looking for, and thanks to Chevy coming through...

With the two blocks of Broadway that separate Bedford-Stuyvesant in Brooklyn up in flames behind them, Paul sprinted down the sidewalk after the fleeing hoodlum who had stolen his satchel.

...I knew exactly where to find him.

The rain had started to let up at this point, but everything was still soaked, and there were countless puddles everywhere as the chase continued. With the leather satchel dangling from his hand, the hood cried out for help that never came before he darted down an alleyway. It was only a matter of time because Paul was quickly closing in on him.

The hood careened out the other side of the alley, and ran directly into traffic, barely avoiding being hit by numerous cars. The traffic was even heavier than normal because the blackout shut down the entire subway system, forcing everyone into alternative travel plans, just to make their commutes home from work. The commute was so bad at one point the Brooklyn Bridge was completely jammed with both cars, as well as pedestrians, who were trying to make their way along the bridge's center walkway.

The hoodlum recklessly maneuvered around the heavy foot and car traffic, managing to put some distance between the two of them. They had been at it for a while already now, with both men swimming in sweat, their legs and lungs on fire, but both of them knew the high stakes of the outcome of this footrace.

"Someone help me!"

He was screaming at the top of his lungs, but still no one seemed to give a shit. Both men darted quickly by two cops, who were too busy with looters they had pinned up against what was left of the front of an A&P supermarket to take notice, so their little game of cat and mouse continued uninterrupted. The hoodlum made it to the other side of the street and started to sprint down the sidewalk. He nearly ate it when he almost ran into a bunch of young kids drinking and playing with water that sprung from a fire hydrant, giving Paul a chance to once again start to catch up—but before he could close the gap completely, the hood quickly ducked behind the next corner.

Paul rounded that same corner but was nearly knocked off of his feet when he had to dodge flames that came roaring out from a storefront window. He managed to shield his eyes from the fire, though, just in time to see the hoodlum duck into another alleyway up ahead.

The hood frantically started to climb up a fire escape, looking down once he was halfway up to see Paul had started up after him. He made it to the top, pulled himself up, and started to sprint again. Paul pulled himself up too, mere seconds behind, his eyes still very much on the prize.

"Stop fucking running!"

Fat chance of that happening, so Paul continued to give chase. Neither man was going to stop, because neither could afford to, so it wasn't much longer before the two of them found themselves jumping from rooftop to rooftop. As their chase took flight, Paul managed to get closer and closer with each of those leaps, and soon he was practically within arm's reach of the man. Seeing his chance, Paul's fingers reached out to grab the back of him, but at the very last minute the hood reached another ledge and managed to jump.

He didn't make it to the next ledge, though. In fact, he wasn't even that close really. Of course, being close wouldn't have really mattered much anyway. This wasn't horseshoes, or hand grenades.

Paul managed to pull up just in time to watch the screaming hood as he fell downward, with his body eventually impaled on a crude metal fence below. As gruesome as the visual was, the sounds of flesh and bone being abruptly pierced and cracked, along with the unnatural groan that escaped the man's lips on impact, was far more haunting.

Paul slowly climbed down a fire escape into the alleyway below, before picking up the hoodlum's knife from the ground and putting it in his pocket. He grabbed the leather satchel next, opening it up to reveal it was still filled with some of the cash. Some of the cash. As satisfied as he was going to get, Paul was about to walk away when he heard the hoodlum.

"Please," the hood gasped, causing Paul to look up to see the man was in horrendous pain but still somehow managing to cling to some semblance of life. Paul hesitated for a moment, before walking over to him and assessing the damage. Maybe this was hand grenades after all.

"You're not going to live through this, no matter what I do, or don't do," Paul finally said, as the hood's eyes started to fill with tears. "I'm sorry," Paul continued, before starting to walk away again, but the hood wasn't ready to relent.

"Please. Don't make me die alone," he pleaded, prompting Paul to nod his head "yes" before returning to the hood's side, taking his hand in his own. The hood groaned some more, struggling to breath, as the tears continued to stream down his face. It was a gruesome scene, but Paul never looked away. He continued to hold the man's hand, actually looking at him with sympathetic and compassion-filled eyes the entire time.

"Thank y–" The hood didn't get to finish, because the life had already escaped from his body, leaving Paul holding the hand of a newly dead man. Part of him actually felt bad for the wayward son, but the memories of the evils he had done to the old man, and the young woman, along with what he had put him through personally by stealing the satchel, quickly set him straight. He held the lifeless hand for another moment, finally letting it go to gently close the man's eyes, before turning and walking away from the departed.

———

Paul once again carried the leather satchel as he made his way through the massive glass doorway of the upscale New York apartment building. He was immediately greeted by the beam of a high-grade flashing in his eyes.

"Don't shoot…It's Paul."

"What are you doing here?"

The question came as the light was slowly lowered, followed by a now heavily-armed doorman stepping forward in the darkness.

"I need to see Chevy."

"He's not here. Won't be back until sometime tomorrow afternoon."

Paul just stood there, contemplating for a beat, before finally responding with, "Okay. Do you have a bag then, and a piece of paper and a pen?"

The doorman couldn't help but to laugh, obviously having a hard time taking Paul's request seriously.

"Come on, man. It can be a trash bag. Doesn't have to be fancy," Paul said, causing the doorman to shake his head in disbelief before he led the way through the darkness with Paul following close behind.

Eventually they found their way to a storage closet nestled strategically between the freight elevators and the loading dock doors. The doorman pulled out a large key ring, overflowing with countless keys, but managed to effortlessly find the key to the door, even in the dark. He unlocked and opened the door, then handed the flashlight to Paul to hold while he stepped inside the small space.

"I'm not sure where you want me to point this thing."

"I don't need it. I know everything that's in here, and where it's at."

So, with the doorman fishing around in a box toward the back of the space, Paul flashed the flashlight beam around the shelves inside toward the front. At first caught his eye, but eventually the beam of light, and Paul's interest were solely on a box of plastic drop-clothes just like the one the doorman had rolled up the bartender's lifeless body in. *No wonder the doorman knew the closet's contents so well*, Paul thought to himself, as the man came out from the darkness. He was carrying a trash bag in his hand and noticed immediately what Paul was looking at.

"There's still a chance you wind up wrapped up in one of those things, you know," he said, with an unnerving smile on his face. Clearly the man got off on pain and violence. He was a real sociopath, but he was far from the first one Paul had met in his life, and at the rate he was going Paul was sure he was far from being the last.

The first sociopath Paul ever met was not long after he arrived at the Long Binh Post in Vietnam. Initially he was thrilled to be arriving there, having been first stationed at Binh Thuy, a significantly smaller base that didn't have nearly the amenities the Long Binh Post offered to U.S. soldiers. That initial thrill would be short lived, though, gone in a matter of moments over a few beers at a bar. The beers and the sudden shift in Paul's excitement both were courtesy of a psycho in uniform named Francis.

The Long Binh Post was strategically located between Saigon and Bien Hoa, and during the war it was the largest U.S. Army base in all of South Vietnam. It may have been strategically located for military purposes, but for the troops that found themselves stationed there during their tour the Long Binh Post offered an endless list of niceties, making those tours a little more bearable, all things considered.

The post offered everything from proper medical facilities, to ample options for recreational activities. For those looking to be active there were swimming pools to swim in, tennis and basketball courts, a bowling alley, and even a driving range. For those looking for fun after the sunset, there were numerous restaurants, bars, nightclubs, and even "strip clubs" that did little to hide the fact that they had more of an a la carte menu to scratch any itch that needed scratching. With everything the Long Binh Post had to offer, Paul thought he had finally gotten some good luck while he was in country, but two nights, and two beers in, Francis had other plans.

Second Lieutenant Francis Raymond Poole was a twenty-two-year-old who was all too happy to leave his little shithole town in Florida to do "his part" for the red, white and blue. Once he was in Nam, he was quick to earn a reputation at enjoying doing "his part" a little too much, thanks to a happy trigger finger and a real penchant to get up close and personal with enemy soldiers. At least initially "his part" was mainly above board, so Francis went about his business with some real unchecked aggression but eventually the joy he took in ending human lives crossed over a big fucking line.

Francis was a member of Charlie Company's 1st Platoon, and he was more than just a passive observer when his platoon arrived in the Son Tinh District in South Vietnam on March 16, 1968, and he was never shy about recanting the details of his involvement in the My Lai Massacre. Those details alone were enough to make even the sturdiest of stomachs turn, but much to Paul's growing horror over those beers, those details were also accompanied with visual aids Francis kept as prideful mementos.

The My Lai Massacre was a war crime that saw the mass murder of somewhere between three hundred and five hundred unarmed South Vietnamese citizens by U.S. Army soldiers from Company C, 1st Battalion, 20th Infantry Regiment and Company B, 4th Battalion, 3rd Infantry Regiment, 11th Brigade, and the 23rd Infantry Division. As if the sheer numbers of victims weren't staggering enough, the who and the how it happened would ultimately prompt global outrage once news of the incident became public knowledge nearly two years after the tragedy.

Victims of the senseless slaughter were men, women, children, and even infants, but the brutality didn't just encompass the deaths of the unarmed civilians, as some of the women and girls as young as twelve were also raped and mutilated before being executed. Francis' eyes lit up when he recanted how countless mothers jumped on and covered their children, initially shielding them as he expended several M16 rifle magazines into a fleeing crowd, but their efforts would be futile when he was done. Francis continued with glee, telling in graphic detail how he waited until those children who could walk on their own eventually tried to get out from under their dead mothers' bodies, only to meet the same fate as he ripped their tiny bodies to shreds with endless streams of gunfire.

Paul felt the room start to spin as he struggled to keep down the last of his beer, while Francis just kept on telling his tale. Paul wondered when he would finish. He also wondered how many other soldiers had heard the horrors of Francis' brutality, but most of all Paul wondered why he never just got up and left the bar. It wasn't like he was being held hostage or anything, and in hindsight, Paul was more than sure that Francis was getting off on watching the color drain from his face as he continued on and on, with no merciful end in sight. When Francis finally did stop talking, though, Paul knew in his heart of hearts the answer as to why he never got up and left, as he looked at the psychopath's trophies that he proudly displayed on the bar top.

Francis was far from the only one to participate in the massacre, as other soldiers killed, raped, and maimed their share of innocent civilians, with very little to no opposition from their fellow soldiers. By and large, a great deal of the bloodshed at the hands of soldiers, who by all accounts were otherwise good men, could partially be blamed on a mob mentality. By the time the killings finally came to an end Charlie Company had a single casualty, and that was only because the soldier shot himself in the foot to avoid taking part in the massacre. Another soldier who saw the horrors of the massacre unfolding on the ground below as he flew over in his helicopter took a less passive approach to his opposition to the killings.

Warrant Officer Hugh Thompson Jr was a helicopter pilot from Company B's 123rd Aviation Battalion, American Division, who took matters into his own hands after making several failed attempts to radio for help, and after witnessing several acts of brutality upon landing the helicopter. Thompson and his crew saw a sergeant from first platoon fire into a ditch filled with bodies, some of which were still moving, before witnessing a woman who was beaten before being shot in the head at point-blank range by another soldier.

After taking off and landing once again, Thompson positioned his helicopter and crew in between a bunker filled with terrified civilians and approaching U.S. soldiers. After facing opposition from an approaching Lieutenant he initially implored to help safely extract the civilians from the bunker, Thompson did it himself, but not before ordering his crew to open fire on the soldiers if they were to fire on the bunker. He was able to safely get more than a dozen civilians to the helicopter before they took to the air to look for more opportunities to help those who couldn't help themselves.

Thompson's actions not only help save lives, but it also helped end the My Lai Massacre, when he reported the atrocities he witnessed to his company commander, Major Frederic W. Watke. Watkewould relay the allegations to LTC Barker, the operations overall commander, and who would start the cease-fire order by radioing his executive officer who was still on the ground. Thompson's efforts wouldn't end there, though, as he would later be interviewed during the subsequent investigations and eventually testify in the military prosecution against those involved. Neither was a quick and easy process, as both were hampered by an internal cover up that included initial reports that claimed more than a hundred Viet Cong and only twenty-two civilians had been killed during a firefight. Stars and Stripes magazine even went so far as to describe the engagement as one that ended with the killing of, "128 Communists in a bloody day-long battle."

For his efforts Thompson was awarded the Distinguished Flying Cross, but he threw the medal away because the citation that came with it included a fabricated account of his heroism during "intense crossfire." He would later receive a Purple Heart, the oldest award still given to members of the U.S. military, which is awarded in the name of the President to personnel that are either wounded or killed during service. Thirty years after the My Lai Massacre, the Army tried to award Thompson the Soldier's Medal, the highest honor awarded for bravery that did not involve direct conflict with the enemy. He initially refused to accept the medal, because the military wanted to award it to him quietly, and Thompson felt that not only should it be done publicly but that his entire crew should be honored as well.

The initial cover up of the My Lai Massacre held strong, at least until Tom Glen, a soldier of the 11th Light Infantry Brigade, wrote a letter to the new MACV (Military Assistance Command Vietnam), where he deftly described how he witnessed the constant brutality against civilians in Vietnam by U.S. soldiers. Glen didn't specifically mention the events of the My Lai Massacre, as he wasn't present for them, but instead his letter spoke of a more universal issue of racial intolerance that he feared plagued the American soldier.

A second letter, independent of the one sent by Glen, was sent to thirty members of Congress. In the letter, Specialist 5 Ronald L. Ridenhour, a door gunner from the 11th Infantry Brigade, imploring them to investigate the "Pinkville incident"—Pinkville was what American soldiers called the small hamlet where the My Lai Massacre occurred because of the reddish-pink color of the location on the topographic maps. Like Glen, Ridenhour hadn't been present at the massacre, but he and his pilot flew over the area days afterwards and witnessed the devastating aftermath of all of the death and destruction.

Neither letter moved many people in power to action, but they certainly lent credibility to what actually did, when the My Lai Massacre finally became public knowledge after a story was published in the Dispatch News Service by freelance journalist Seymour Hersh on November 13, 1969. It had taken nearly two years from when the incident occurred, but after the piece was out there, there'd be no more keeping this quiet, despite frantic, but failed, efforts by the Nixon administration for damage control and containment.

Twenty-six men would eventually face charges for the My Lai Massacre, and during the four-month trial, Lieutenant William Calley Jr. constantly claimed he was merely following the orders of his commanding officer. Despite what he considered a justifiable defense, Calley was still found guilty of committing premeditated murder of at least twenty people, and was sentenced to life in prison. It was a sentence that seemed almost from the get-go to be short lived, as President Nixon inexplicably had Calley released from Fort Benning and put under house arrest instead while he awaited the results of an appeal.

His appeals would be denied, but in the end, Calley would end up only serving three-and-a-half years under house arrest at Fort Benning before he was paroled toward the end of 1974 by the Secretary of the Army, Howard Callaway. He would be the one and only person of the twenty-six that were charged to be found guilty, and just like that, less than four years of an initial life sentence, justice for the hundreds of innocent men, women, and children who were killed was no more.

Like the rest of the world, Paul followed the trial and conviction. He had never met Lieutenant William Calley Jr. or any of the other twenty-five men who faced charges, but one thing he was sure of was that none of them were as evil or psychotic as the man he shared those beers with at the bar at the Long Binh Post. If there was any doubt about that at any point during their encounter, that doubt was long gone after Francis opened the pages of the 1965 Playboy Magazine with Playmate of the Year Jo Collins on the cover.

Paul knew the issue well, as did most American G.I.s, because Playboy Magazine had quickly become an avid part of the Vietnam War for several reasons. A good deal of the publication's popularity amongst serving military members was, of course, because of its content, both the numerous photos of the beautiful nude women as well as the magazine's focus on tackling the numerous controversial issues of the times. But there was even more to it than what was between the pages. The magazine and its founder, Hugh Hefner, an

Army veteran himself, were always vocal supporters of the troops, which spilled over to them openly encouraging their readers to support those who were serving their country even if they didn't necessarily support the war itself.

That particular issue became legendary to those serving thanks to Lieutenant Jack Price of the 173rd Airborne's 503rd Infantry Regiment. Prior to the issue being released, Playboy had launched a rather adventurous promotional offer, one that promised that the first issue of a lifetime subscription would be delivered, in person, by a Playboy playmate for $150. When Lieutenant Price and other members of his battalion came up with the cash, it certainly made the hand delivery a little more difficult than the marketing team at Playboy had anticipated.

With Price stationed over in Vietnam, Jo Collins, who would eventually be aptly and fondly known as G.I. Jo, had quite the trek to follow through on the promotion, but she would make the last leg of the trip by way of a Bell UH-1 helicopter, better known as a Huey. Thanks to a gunshot wound, she would hand Price the issue while he was lying in a hospital bed at the Bien Hoa air base, while the other men of his company would have to wait to meet her until the end of their most recent of countless bloody battles with Vietcong soldiers. The company was nicknamed "Bloody Bravo" because of those countless bloody battles, but even more so because of the countless casualties they seemed to sustain during them.

The cover of the issue with G.I. Jo on it that Francis was holding was well worn, as a lot of the copies of that issue would be for obvious reasons. The copy lying on the bar in front of Paul was well worn for other reasons, though, with an evil and putrid bastardization of something near and dear to American soldiers now making up the pages that were inside that worn cover.

Thanks to authorization by President John F. Kennedy in 1962, enlisted soldiers that were part of the DASPO (Department of the Army's Special Photographic Office) were sent to the Vietnam war with cameras. More than two hundred enlisted men were up for the task of capturing an honest, and oftentimes harsh, view of the war over the span of ten-plus years. Because of the need to be mobile in a hurry, and to be able maneuver in tight spaces quickly with a camera in tow, many of these soldier photographers went without the added safety of wearing helmets and other protective gear. They were also barely armed, with both sacrifices for their own wellbeing meaning not all of them made it home alive.

One such unfortunate member of the DASPO took his last breath with Second Lieutenant Francis Raymond Poole standing over him. True to form, good ole Francis ignored the man's pleas for morphine, instead choosing to focus his attention on the dying man's camera, and the unused rolls of Tri-X film. The first photographs that Second Lieutenant Francis Raymond Poole would ever take in his life would be of the dying soldier photographer at his feet, but those photographs were nothing more than a warm up for a sociopath with a new hobby. The true bulk of that new hobby would find its way on the majority of those rolls of Tri-X film on March 16, 1968,. The subsequent photographs were then taped inside the pages of that well-worn 1965 issue of Playboy Magazine, with playmate Jo Collins on the front cover.

Paul sat there, completely shell shocked and unable to move or speak, as Francis turned page after page of the magazine, proudly showing off photograph after photograph of mutilated women and young children from the My Lai Massacre. As if the grotesque photographs weren't already disturbing enough, each one came with a trophy that Francis had collected from each dead body. Next to each photograph, a handful or so of black hair was neatly pinned, all except for one, which Francis was quick to explain. When he had finished with the explanation, every ounce of Paul's being had wished he had just stayed mum on the missing hair.

In his unsolicited explanation, Francis made it a point to say that the young girl, who he had put at around fourteen or fifteen years old, had no head to take the hairs from, so he had to improvise. He said he knew her to be about that age, because he knew she had at least reached puberty, and that although it was hard to see at first, clearly he had collected some hair and taped it next to her photograph—but it wasn't hair from head.

Francis was never charged with any crimes for his involvement in the My Lai Massacre, but it wasn't for lack of evidence, as that issue of Playboy and another one just like it were eventually found by members of the 18th Military Police Brigade when they searched his belongings. Francis was never charged with anything, because Francis never made it back to that shithole town in Florida where he'd grown up. His body was found hanging from a rafter, three days after that night in the bar with Paul. Aside from the noose around his neck, toxicology reporters would later show that he had enough heroin in his system to kill a small horse.

Scoring that much heroin was easy, as the drug had started to flow more freely into Vietnam from Cambodia after that country's civil war in 1970. Paul also didn't have much trouble getting close enough to Francis, and getting him to shoot up, either. Their little bonding time over beers at the bar provided enough trust between them, and by the time Francis had mentioned he had a second magazine filled with more photos and more strands of hair under his mattress, Paul had already made up his mind about what had to be done. Now he had his opening, and he was quick to take it.

Francis didn't think anything of the fact Paul had brought two syringes with him, especially after Paul explained he just wasn't a fan of sharing needles. He'd be too high to do anything about it once he found out the real reason for the second syringe. Francis just looked at Paul, his eyes glazed over and a confused look on his face, as Paul shot the second hit into psycho's vein. At one point Francis tried to stand up, but wound up falling to the floor instead. He went in and out of consciousness a few times while Paul injected him with two more doses of junk. Paul knew that three were probably more than enough, but he wanted to be sure that the monster at his feet would never be able to kill again.

Paul also knew that a U.S. soldier overdosing would probably be sufficient enough to keep any inquiring minds from digging too deep into Francis' death, but again he wanted to be sure. What he hadn't thought through entirely was how difficult it was going to be, getting a six foot, two-hundred-pound man, who was now literally dead weight, up and hanging from an electrical cord.

It would take him nearly forty minutes to stage the hanging, and another thirty minutes to make sure he removed any trace he had ever even been in Francis' place. It was almost morning by the time Paul had meticulously wiped down the entire place, before finally leaving under the cover of the waning darkness. He showered and was in his own bed just as the sun started to peak over the horizon, confident that he had pulled this off and that the world was a better place now because of it.

As far as the United States Army and the United States Government were concerned, though, Second Lieutenant Francis Raymond Poole never even existed. So, even if Paul had accidentally left behind any evidence, although he was quite sure he had not, it was more than likely that the United States Army's cleanup job would have wiped up anything suggesting it wasn't a suicide.

Making the whole ugly problem just go away wasn't exactly justice for the innocents who lost their lives, but neither was the sham of the trials back in the states for those who were officially charged with a crime. Paul imagined the two Playboy Magazines with the photos and hair trophies disappearing as quickly as they were found, burned up in some fire pit along with anything and everything else that belonged to Francis. He imagined the flames would see to it, that everything that was once a part of that monster would eventually go up in smoke, rendered harmless and soon to be forgotten completely.

As Paul lay in his bed that night, he wished that he too could forget everything that was Francis Raymond Poole, but he knew otherwise. He knew some memories would linger on inside him forever, a painful internal scarring to go along nicely with outward scarring from the bullet wounds that lined his back.

Paul looked back toward the building. The doorman lingered inside in the darkness, still watching him through the glass. He wasn't Francis Raymond Poole, but Paul couldn't help but to wonder if he kept any souvenirs before dumping the endless bodies he had disposed of for Chevy over the years. He wouldn't put it past him, but if he did, no one would ever know about it. A few years later, just like Francis Raymond Poole, someone would take care of the doorman. It wouldn't be pretty. It wouldn't be quick. It wasn't the authorities. Paul wondered if it had been the competition, or perhaps Chevy himself needing to tie up some loose ends to protect his own ass.

More than anything, though, Paul wondered how close he had been to being reduced to a bloody mess, left for that psychopath to cut up into chunks of flesh and bone, before disposing of those pieces. The way the doorman just kept staring at him, Paul couldn't help but to think that maybe that was still a possibility, but he knew he couldn't worry about that now. He still had things he needed to do and he was running out of time to do them.

Paul checked Grand Central Station to see if the trains were running yet. They weren't, but that didn't keep commuters from continuing to wait. There were a lot of them too. Some sat in the empty ticket windows, while others sat on the ground around the information kiosk between track twenty-eight and Vanderbilt Hall, below the famous opal-faced clock.

Designed by Hendry Bedford of the Self Winding Clock Company, the Grand Central Station clock had become a popular meeting spot for New Yorkers over the years, with someone only having to say "Meet me at the clock" as a universal reference for location. The Seth Thomas Clock Company made the movements.

Paul stood and stared at the clock. Despite the blackout, the clock's time was still accurate. Unlike the lingering commuters, Paul couldn't wait around for the power to come back on, and for the trains to start again, so he left the station and continued on his way on foot.

Despite the darkness, and late hour, the streets were littered with trash and others making their way on foot. For some New Yorkers, the blackout didn't even ruin their evening plans, as he passed various bars that were still serving patrons. The Plaza Hotel's famous Palm Court actually managed to continue their dinner service by candlelight. Paul passed by another food venue, The Burger Bistro, that wasn't as successful on the food front, but still managed to stay open, with a chalk-written sign out front that said, "No lights, No Food, but lots of Liquor." The sign seemed to have worked, as the place was packed with people and overflowing with drunken laughter.

Not all businesses were as interested in keeping patronage during the blackout, though, and rightfully so, as parts of the city continued to burn, and the sounds of police and fire truck sirens still filled the air. After a while, Paul didn't even hear them, as he pushed on through the darkness. Before long, he started to make his way through a working-class neighborhood along the waterfront in Brooklyn. It was a rough area that had fallen on hard times, and those hard times had only gotten worse as the textile mills that had provided jobs along the Bushwick/East Williamsburg border started to close. The Rheingold plant by Flushing and Bushwick Avenues was the last to close a year before the blackout.

To add insult to injury, those who had power would use it to exploit those who were already suffering. Banks and realtors used the troubling times to run a mortgage scam in the area, where they would file fraudulent paperwork for buyers who had no real way to afford to buy, to get the federally backed Federal Housing Administration loans for insurance on the unstable mortgages. Once the low-income buyer could no longer afford to pay, they would default, and those in power would clean up on the insurance payment.

With hundreds of abandoned buildings now populating the neighborhood, local politicians started to ignore the need for financial resources for upkeep of the mostly wood-framed buildings. The neglect, along with cutting back on other public resources like firefighters, would ultimately lead to countless fires in the area. During the blackout forty-five businesses along the commercial strip below the J train tracks went up in flames, but it wouldn't end when the lights came back on. A few days later, the "All Hands Fire" started in an abandoned factory and wouldn't stop until it took out twenty-three other nearby buildings.

Even on normal nights, Bushwick wasn't the safest of neighborhoods to be walking through, but that had never stopped Paul in the past and it wasn't about to stop him now. After all, one of the things he still needed to do was in this neighborhood, and he was running out of time to do it.

Two shotgun-wielding barflies stood guard outside a rundown bar. They passed a bottle between them, drinking liberally with each turn, apparently neither really phased by the power-outage. They were neighborhood boys, who had grown up into blue-collared neighborhood men. At one point in their lives, their binge drinking would have been reserved for the hours between shifts at the Rheingold plant. These days and nights, though, the booze had become more of a full-time gig for them. By the looks of things, tonight they had been working double time. Like a lot of the neighborhood boys, neither of them would ever travel outside of New York City, and just like the others, they were more than okay with that fact. Their neighborhood, for all of its faults, was always loyal to them. For all of their shortcomings, they were also always loyal to their neighborhood, and tonight was certainly no different as one of them spotted someone approaching in the darkness.

"That's close enough," one of them called out, as they quickly put the bottle down, and raised their guns toward the approaching stranger. The person approaching didn't stop. "I promise you, we'll shoot!"

"As if either of you could see straight at this point," Paul said as he emerged from the darkness, his hands in the air, and the leather satchel over his shoulder. "Is Vicky here?"

"She is," Vicky replied, as she stepped out from the doorway. "He's fine, boys." The barflies lowered their weapons, allowing Paul to lower his hands. "What are you doing here?"

"What can I say, I missed seeing your beautiful smile." The remark caused her to cackle, the moonlight showcasing her unsightly teeth.

"You want a drink, wiseass?"

"Only if you're buying, you old hag."

"Good to see that despite the fact that we're in the middle of a city-wide blackout, you're still as cheap as ever. You know this is going to hurt my business, don't you?"

"Half your customers already don't even pay, Vicky."

"Yeah, I don't think I'll be making the Fortune 500 anytime soon, but you know this bar was never really about making money."

She was right. Paul knew she owned and ran the bar for reasons that went beyond financial, both because she had told him as much, and from his own personal experiences with running up a hefty tab. Vicky was also right about the blackout hurting businesses, though, even if she wasn't worried about her own establishment.

Mayor Beame and other New York City officials estimated that the cost to businesses in the city was upwards of $150 million from the theft and property damage alone. They believed it to be in the hundreds of millions in total amount of losses from the lost workday. That didn't even take into consideration possible losses on a global scale from Wall Street closing down as well. Fortunately for Vicky's bar, there'd be no theft or damages, so she and Paul were left to focus on what really mattered in life.

Over candlelight, Vicky poured Paul a drink, before pouring one for herself. Under different circumstances, with two different people, the setup would have made for one hell of a romantic setting. This, like the rest of their relationship, wasn't really about romance, at least not in the traditional sense. What they shared was pure and authentic, and just being around her and the bar brought with it a certain level of comfort that Paul couldn't find anywhere else. Despite that much needed, and much appreciated, comfort he was still carrying with him everything he had going on. He did little to hide this, and like always, Vicky was quick to notice when he was down.

"Not going to lie. I've missed having mopey Paul around."

"Well, you're in luck, because mopey Paul is here to happily oblige," he replied, as they clinked their glasses before drinking.

"So what, you need a friendly ear, mopey Paul?"

"Nope. Just a refill," he said, as he lit up a smoke, while she refilled both of their glasses.

"Let me get one of those."

"I thought you quit."

She reached out and took the one right out of his mouth, and started to smoke it.

"Whole fucking city's gone mad, so I'd say smoking is the least of my potential problems, love."

"Speaking of madness, I have to say I'm seriously doubting your choice of security."

Vicky puffed on what was left of his cigarette, as her eyes slowly drifted toward a window by the front door and found the silhouettes of the two shotgun-wielding barflies outside, before returning her attention to Paul.

"It's more for show. Everyone in the neighborhood knows this place is... protected," she said, lingering on that last word as her mind drifted off somewhere else, and although he couldn't be certain, it looked as if she was on the verge of shedding a tear or two.

"You okay?"

Whatever emotion was coming, was quickly washed back down with the remainder of her drink.

"He's been gone for years, but they still look out for me, you know. Two of them have been sitting in a car on the corner since the power went out."

"Black Fleetwood?"

She nodded her head before pouring them both another round. Paul had seen the two guys she was talking about on his walk up to the bar. Two typical wiseguys, parked in a pristine, jet black, 1976 Cadillac Fleetwood.

I don't know, maybe I'm getting soft in my old age, but it's kinda nice. Being looked out for like that, even after all these years."

Paul didn't know how to respond, at least not about her fondness for those offering personal security, especially considering the circumstances that brought the need for that security to come to fruition. He decided instead to just shift the conversation away from the topic all together.

"The madness will pass. Once the lights come back on, everyone will go back to the way they were before."

"And does that include you, Paul?"

Paul lit up another cigarette for himself, his mind racing as he looked down at the satchel that was at his side.

"That depends on what happens at noon today," he replied, as he polished off his drink. When he was finished, he turned to her, so that the two of them were left just looking at one another.

"Then I think you should dance with me," she said, prompting Paul to look over at the lifeless jukebox.

"I'm not an electrician, but I don't think your jukebox is working."

We've danced together enough over the years," she said, as she got up from the barstool, and took him by the hand. "I'm sure if we really want to, we could hear the music from all of those memories."

They sure did have a lot of memories between them, Paul thought to himself as she led him to their usual spot, laying her head on his shoulder as they started to dance, the sounds of sirens in the distance the closest thing they had to music. At one point in time, Paul wouldn't have dared dance with Vicky, because back then no one would have danced with her and lived to tell about it.

The bar had been a neighborhood staple going on more than three decades. The old and faded sign above the front door of the place said "*Marion & Vincent's*" with one half of the name coming from the place's original owner. He also just so happened to be who Vicky referred to as her second "husband." Vincent wasn't exactly one to focus on the bar's day-to-day operations when he took over the rights to the building in 1946, though, because Vincent was busy with the day-to-day operations of another kind of business.

Vincenzo Giovanni Mangano was a Sicilian born on March 28, 1888 in Palermo, Italy. In 1908, Vincenzo and his brother Philip, arrived in New York City while working on a freighter ship. The two of them would never leave, instead choosing to desert their jobs on the ship in order to illegally enter the United States. The brothers started as nobodies, working as longshoremen on the Brooklyn waterfront, but by 1931 Vincent would be named the head of one of the modern five families after Salvatore Maranzano's victory in the Castellammarese War.

What was previously known as the Mineo family at the time, would eventually be known as the Gambino family, joining the Bonanno, Colombo, Genovese, and Lucchese families, as the five major New York City organized crime families of the Italian American Mafia. Having finally come out on top of a bloody power struggle between himself and Joe 'The Boss" Masseria that lasted a little over a year, Maranzano formed the five families and appointed himself as *cap di tutti capi* (boss of all bosses), with the expectations that each of the family's bosses would report directly to him. Someone had other ideas, though, and less than six months later, four government agents were sent to Maranzano's office at 230 Park Avenue in Manhattan.

It wasn't until his men were disarmed by the four men that Maranzano realized they were not, in fact, government agents, but by then it was too late. To add insult to injury, Tommy Lucchese, one of the other heads of the five families, was there to point out Maranzano to the hired Jewish gangsters, who subsequently stabbed him repeatedly, before finally shooting him.

Maranzano's execution came by orders of Charles "Lucky" Luciano, who set the hit in motion in order to prevent his own death, which had been ordered by Maranzano. The assassination marked the end of the *capo di tutti capi* title, as Luciano established a more diplomatic arrangement in its place. The Commission was a ruling committee that consisted of the bosses of the Five Families of New York, the bosses out of Chicago, as well as those from the Buffalo crime family.

The Gambino family had a highly profitable racket centered around the Brooklyn waterfront and aided by their control over the Brooklyn Local 1814 of the International Longshoremen's Association. With the Commission in place, and as one of the five heads, Vincent had his seat at the table—but it was an entirely different seat that he'd been sitting in when he first laid eyes on Vicky.

Vicky didn't always go by the name Vicky Roberts, and she wasn't always just an aging wisecracker who tended bar either. She had the newspaper clippings and old photographs stashed away behind the bar as proof on both accounts. She used to have them proudly on display, but at some point she decided her colorful past was better left under less of a spotlight, hence the name change from Marion Strasmick to the far more bland and forgettable Vicky Roberts. She still took those old clippings out and showed them from time to time, though, but only for those patrons who she felt close enough to trust with that fading part of her life. Naturally, Paul had seen them on more than one occasion, and after the first time he did, he wasn't surprised that she got the attention of a guy like Vincent Mangano, even if he was already married with kids.

Marion's life started simple enough, growing up in a small suburb of Boston, but by the time she was a teen, the lure of shining on stage became too intoxicating, and far too bright for that small town. She was off to New York City, with dreams of becoming a famous dancer glissading around inside her head, and before long she would have the attention of America's most renowned impresario, Florenz "Flo" Ziegfield.

Over the course of twenty-plus years, any dancer who was lucky enough to be one of Ziegfield's girls, in either his yearly follies, or in one of his shows on Broadway, would consider it a career-defining achievement. For those fortunate few, being a part of something that Ziegfield put together even once would mean that they had reached the pinnacle of their careers. Marion, and more importantly Ziegfield, knew she was far from being just any old dancer, though, so she appeared in eighteen performances of the show "Rio Rita." Ziegfield hadn't wanted their professional collaboration to stop at the eighteen shows, as the run of show was nearly five hundred performances—an extremely long run for a show at that time—but sometimes life has a way of quickly changing one's priorities and that would certainly be the case for Marion.

Originally the show premiered at the new Ziegfeld Theater, but it would later move to the Lyric Theatre, before Marion, now going by the name Marion "Kiki" Roberts, ended up joining the show at its final stop, at the Majestic Theatre on 245 West 44th Street in Manhattan. The last venue for the production was far from some sort of downgrade, as the Majestic was one of the largest theaters on Broadway with 1,681 seats. In one of those 1,681 seats, on Marion's fourteenth of her eventual eighteen performances, sat the future love of her life.

Vincent would also attend the fifteen, sixteen, seventeenth, and her final performance of the show, sitting in premium seats each and every night. If anyone had cared enough to ask him what the show was actually about, he'd have no idea, though, as his eyes never left Marion throughout each and every one of those performances, as well as during their drinks that followed each night after she wrapped. The last night they'd share a hotel room after those drinks, and Marion would resign from the show the next morning.

At this point in life, both Vincent and Marion were both married, but those marriages couldn't have been more different from one another. Vincent had been married to Carolina Cusimano in Brooklyn for more than ten years and the couple had four children together. By all accounts, it was a happy and fruitful marriage, and Carolina would remain fiercely loyal to her husband, even after the rumors started.

As for Marion, she married to a Greek immigrant not long after she arrived in New York City. He came from humble beginnings before arriving in the United States, and those humble beginnings had carried over to him being a waiter who lived a simple life in Astoria, Queens. Her hunger for the limelight, and his preference for a more common lifestyle, put their marriage at odds almost immediately. By the time she met Vincent, their marriage still existed merely just to save face around the neighborhood, and he wasn't exactly the first gangster that she had fancied.

Jack "Legs" Diamond, also known as "Gentleman Jack," was an Irish American gangster who ran with the likes of Arnold Rothstein, and at one time actually served as Rothstein's personal bodyguard. Unlike Marion's husband, and his own wife, Legs lived a rather lavished and even celebrity lifestyle at the time. His fame and notoriety made him a beloved figure to the public, as well as the countless women he slept with, but he also had a lot of enemies, which brought about numerous arrests by the authorities as well as countless failed assassination attempts on his life.

Marion knew Jack was living on borrowed time, so although she was heartbroken, she wasn't really surprised to hear that he was killed. It was late December when two gunmen entered his room in Albany, New York the night after he was acquitted on kidnapping charges, and one held him down while the other shot him three times in the back of the head.

There was no shortage of motives for the murder, with the likes of Dutch Schultz, the local police department, and even the Democratic Party Chairman, Dan O' Connell, as possible suspects, but no charges were ever brought against anyone. He'd be buried six days later with around two hundred people in attendance. Gangster molls were practically an accepted part of mob life, but there was still a certain level of reverence given to a man's actual wife, so out of respect for her, Marion wasn't in attendance that day. She did say her goodbyes, though, in private the very next day, when no one else was around.

A gangster's moll, also known as a gun moll or mob moll, was the term used for the mistress of a professional criminal. Marion always hated the term, and hated being referred to as one with Legs and later with Vincent Mangano. Other molls didn't seem to mind, and some even seemed to embrace it, along with the lifestyle that came with the title. Some of the women were, or became, criminals themselves, and some of them paid the ultimate price for being dance partners with those who danced the dance of crime and violence.

The most famous of the gangster molls was Virginia Hill, who went from an Alabama farm girl to eventually being known as the Queen of the gangster molls. She was once the girlfriend of Giuseppe Antonio Doto, better known as Joe Adonis, after Virginia gave him the nickname Adonis, after the Greek God of beauty and desire, because of his good looks and extreme vanity about those looks. Joe Adonis ran a bootlegging operation during Prohibition with Lucky Luciano, Meyer Lansky, and Bugsy Siegel. He was also an influential and important participant in the formation of the modern mafia crime families. Like Marion, though, Virginia was linked to more than one mobster, with her second squeeze running in the same circles as Adonis but far more famous and far more infamous.

Virginia Hill and Bugsy Siegel had a torrid love affair while they were both still in New York City, but it was put on pause when Siegel relocated with his wife and kids to the West Coast. The pause between them would be a short one, though, as their affair started back up again in 1942 after Hill moved to Hollywood in the hopes of getting discovered. Rumors had it that the fights between them were just as fiery as their time together between the sheets, but still, she'd remain his most steady and prized mistress from that point forward, right up until the day he died in her Beverly Hills home.

Another rumor about the two was that Siegel named the Flamingo in Vegas after Hill, because that was his nickname for Virginia. The nickname was, in fact, a wink and a nod between the two of them that was a reference to her exceptional oral sex skills. The fact that the Flamingo was the reason Siegel was killed, and that he was killed in its namesake's home, certainly lent itself a certain amount of irony.

A few days before a .30-caliber, military M1 carbine rifle was fired several times through a window in her home, killing Siegel while he was reading a copy of the Los Angeles Times, Virginia Hill was told to get the hell out of town and don't look back by the kind of people out of New York that exactly didn't mince their words. No one was ever charged for the murder.

Hill did exactly what she was advised to do, but it was only a matter of time before the authorities caught up with her anyway, and she was subpoenaed to testify at the Kefauver hearings in 1951, where she remained faithful to the cause and denied knowing anything about organized crime. Her loyalty wouldn't exactly be rewarded, though, as she spent her remaining days living in Europe to avoid being indicted for failure to pay income taxes, before she was silenced for good when she died under mysterious circumstances. Her cause of death was ruled a suicide from overdosing on sleeping pills, but those in the know might wisely suggest otherwise.

Virginia Hill was far from the only gangster's moll to live and die by the sword, with countless others either ending up serving time, being killed, or doing both in some cases. Janice Drake's love affair with mobster Anthony Carfano would end with both of them shot to death by two Genovese hitmen. Bonnie Parker of Bonnie and Clyde fame would meet her maker when the car they were in was lit up with gunfire from the authorities, killing them both by the time it was all over. John Dillinger's girl, Evelyn "Billie" Frechette, would end up serving two years in jail for harboring a criminal, and was still behind bars when he was shot and killed by the FBI. Helen Gillis would turn herself in after her husband Baby Face Nelson was killed by police, and would serve time for her involvement in his gang.

These were just a handful of examples of how being a gangster moll wasn't always glamorous, and how more times than not, it was short lived and ended badly. Marion knew all of this, but she didn't care. She was willing to risk everything, because she truly loved Vincent Giovanni Mangano and he truly loved her back. He treated her like a queen, and she treated him like he was an actual person, which he adored about their relationship. For most of Vincent's life, especially after he came into some power, he never really knew who was being authentic with him. But that was never the case when it came to Marion, because from day one she was never afraid to put him in his place. She loved him unconditionally, but with that she would never hesitate to tell him when he was wrong. Where most people saw and rightfully feared Vincent "The Executioner," Marion always just saw Vincent the man, and for that he trusted her emphatically, which wasn't something he could say about anyone else outside of his brother, who also happened to be his consigliere.

Most of Vincent's days were dedicated to his wife and family, and of course his business, but once the sun would set, if there was no more need to do business, his nights usually belonged to Marion. It never really mattered to Marion what they would do, but most of those nights together were spent as if they were ripped right out of the pages of a fairytale. Some nights they'd head out to Harlem, and get the finest seats in the house while they listen to legendary jazz performers like Cab Calloway, Billie Holiday, and Duke Ellington at The Cotton Club. Other nights they'd head over to 10 East 60th Street to rub elbows with Hollywood celebrities at mob boss Frank Costello's Copacabana. Other nights they'd dine on the porterhouse for two at Broadway's first steakhouse. Gallagher's Steakhouse was originally a speakeasy during Prohibition, but after Prohibition ended, owners Helen Gallagher and Jack Solomon converted it into the first restaurant to serve the New York Strip cut.

Almost every night would end with them arriving at the Grand Central Terminal and checking in to the Presidential Suite at The Biltmore Hotel. Vincent preferred the Biltmore over other options like the Ritz-Carlton on Madison Avenue at West 46th Street, or the Hotel Astor on Broadway between 44th and 45th Streets, mainly because it had a private elevator to the Presidential Suite. He also wasn't shy about his adoration of the Italian gardens that sat on top of the towers, overlooking Vanderbilt Avenue and Grand Central Terminal. In the winter, the gardens were turned into an ice-skating rink. Vincent didn't skate, but Marion sure did, and she was incredibly graceful, which was certainly something he enjoyed watching.

Having lived through Prohibition, Marion joked one time what their plan would be should they bring Prohibition back because they both enjoyed drinking so much. Vincent's response was to buy a small bar, and Marion & Vincent's was born. He obviously enjoyed spoiling her every chance he had, which she was well aware of, but in his mind, she was the one who spoiled him. Ultimately, they both just agreed that they spoiled each other, and for years they'd both continue to do so.

Like most affairs, the earlier days of theirs were far better than the later ones, but not because of how they felt about one another. When she met Vincent, he was at the height of his mob boss days, with the Mangano family in total control of the waterfront, in good part due to Anthony Anastasio being a member of the family as well as the president of the Brooklyn Local 1814. The most prosperous times for the family were when Vincent and Anastasio were on the same page with one another, and just as importantly with the heads of the other families. For most of his rise, and subsequent time as the family head, Vincent enjoyed a good relationship with the other bosses, but tension eventually grew around loyalties between the other families and Anastasio.

Adding to Vincent's stress was the growing split between the families over the direction of the Italian Mafia, particularly when it came to selling narcotics, which was only compounded by a natural divide between new blood wanting to change from the ways of the past. Vincent Mangano was old school, and his allegiances were in alignment with the old school ways, which directly conflicted with Anastasio's desire to usher in the new era. Naturally, all that stress took a toll on Vincent's personal life, his relationship with Marion included, although she continued to offer her support in any way possible.

In keeping with her way, she was far from being in the dark on Mangano's business from day one, which meant she was up to speed on the growing tensions he was facing with Anastasio. As always, she wasn't shy about offering her honest and unfiltered perspective on things, which in this case happened to be in direct opposition to the advice being given of his brother, as well as Vincent's own opinion on the matter. Marion saw the writing on the wall, and understood that delaying change would just be delaying the inevitable, because she knew that it would happen with or without Vincent being along for the ride. For the first time in their relationship, she even took to begging and pleading for him to listen to her reasoning, but her best efforts were still not enough.

Vincent and Philip Mangano stuck to their guns, and on April 19, 1951, they would both go missing. Later that same day, Philip was found in a marshland area of the Jamaica Bay area of Brooklyn. A woman who was fishing off her boat discovered his lifeless body, with one bullet wound in his neck and two in his face. Despite an extensive search, Vincent's body was never found, and he was declared dead in absentia on October 30, 1961. No one was ever charged with either brother's death, and the man who was most likely behind both, Albert Anastasia, would take over as the head of the family in Vincent's absence.

Marion never ended up serving any time behind bars. She didn't mysteriously die from overdosing on sleeping pills, and she certainly didn't get shot to death by any of Vincent's enemies, or by the authorities. Instead, her tale of being a gangster moll ended more along the lines of the way Kathryn Kelly's did, although their stories' ending was pretty much the only commonality between the two of them. Kathryn was the better half of George Kelly Barnes, better known as Machine Gun Kelly, and unlike Marion, she actively participated in crime. After a successful criminal run with her husband that consisted mainly of bootlegging and kidnapping for ransom, Kathryn ended up serving hard time for her involvement. It was the path she chose to follow after she was released that Marion intentionally ended up emulating. When the FBI finally caught up to them, Machine Gun Kelly, his wife Kathryn, and her mother would all be convicted and sentenced to life in prison. Machine Gun Kelly would spend seventeen years of his sentence in Alcatraz as inmate number 117, before being transferred to Leavenworth Prison in 1951. He died there, attacked on his 59th birthday, on July 18, 1954. Kathryn and her mother would eventually be released, after serving twenty-five years at a women's correctional facility in West Virginia. Kathryn changed her name to Lera Cleo Kelly, and spent the rest of her life as a bookkeeper in Oklahoma City.

Marion was never threatened after Vincent disappeared. Despite the fact that those who were most likely responsible for his disappearance openly looked out for her and the bar over the years, she had learned enough from the likes of other gangster molls who did things the wrong way and who were ultimately silenced because of it. So, once it was clear that he was missing for good, Marion decided to get in front of any need to be silenced, and followed in Kathryn Kelly's footsteps. Marion disappeared, in essence, with Vincent, by changing her name to Vicky Roberts, ostensibly ending the story of Marion and Vincent for good, and starting a whole new tale.

"So, how's your new book coming along?"

"I'm almost done actually," Paul replied. "Just need to find the ending." They continued to dance in the dark without music, but it didn't matter, because it just worked between them.

"You know what would make a great ending?" she said with a wicked smile.

"Please don't say it," Paul said, shaking his head.

"What? All I know is that the sun will be up soon, and if there ever was a time for us to fuck, this would be it," she said anyway.

"Wouldn't your two boyfriends outside get jealous?"

"Eh, monogamy is overrated," she replied, still smiling.

"One day you're going to make some lucky boy truly happy, Vicky."

She pulled him in closer, and he didn't resist. It was a sincere and touching moment between two true friends. Vicky couldn't help thinking about those she had loved and lost when she was still Marion, and she wished more than anything not to lose someone she loved now as Vicky. "I sure hope this isn't our last dance, Paul."

"Yeah...me too. Me too."

MANHATTAN: Thursday July 14th

DAWN ON JULY 14, 1977 looked like none other Paul had ever seen in the city, as he stood and looked at the Manhattan skyline, completely void of lights because of the blackout. There was an eerie calm that had settled in, both city-wide and in Paul as he stepped over broken glass from several shattered windows on his way to his favorite table inside Bickford's Coffee Shop. The place was scarcely populated for once, with the majority of the patrons exhausted police officers, firefighters, and paramedics who were doing their best to unwind after a night for the ages. Paul clutched the leather satchel as he took a seat, and immediately looked up at the clock. It was almost eleven-thirty.

"You waiting for someone?"

Paul looked up as the waitress poured him a cup of coffee.

"Nope. Not today."

"Oh yeah? Where's your girlfriend, Paul?"

"She was just a friend, and...and she...she passed away last night," he replied, causing Linda to cover her mouth, her face red from shame and embarrassment.

"Oh my God, I'm...I'm so sorry. I shouldn't have said that like that," she managed to get out, before covering her mouth again.

"It's okay. You didn't know."

"Are you okay?" she asked, as she took a seat next to him, her face still red. "I think so."

Paul managed to force a smile, not really sure whether or not he really was okay, but the one thing he was sure of was that he was ready for this part of their conversation to pass as quickly as possible.

"Look, if you need anything, let me know," she said, as she placed a hand on his leg, half innocent, half on the verge of crossing a line, with the latter making Paul noticeably uncomfortable. "Anything at all."

"Actually, I'm just glad you guys are open," Paul replied, his eyes focused on her hand.

"Yeah, well we got power back about an hour ago, maybe ten-thirty or so, and the owner thought if we opened there'd be no more vandalism to the place."

"Yeah. Saw those broken windows."

Paul took her hand off of his leg, moving his attention to her eyes, but she quickly looked away from his gaze. She looked devastated.

"I'm sorry. Did I do something wrong?"

"How old are you, Linda?" he asked. The question made her more uncomfortable than she already was, and caused her to take to doing some nervous busy work, mainly of wiping down his table with a washcloth.

"Old enough," got no response from Paul, as he just continued to stare at her, waiting for her to cough up some kind of quantifiable answer. "I'm eighteen, okay? Why do you care?"

"How old are you really?"

"You know what, I don't need this," she said, before abruptly getting up from the table in a huff.

"Calm down. I came here to see you today," he said, his words actually causing her to calm down, and in a hurry.

"Yeah, well you sure have an odd way of showing it."

"Because it's not like that," Paul said, causing her to shake her head "no."

"I've seen the way you look at me, Paul."

Her response left an awkward silence between the two of them for a moment, if for no other reason than for the fact Paul knew she was right. Linda had caught his fancy the moment he first laid eyes on her, and he'd be lying to himself if he didn't know right then and there that she most likely wasn't anything close to legal. In that initial moment, though, and the many similar moments that would follow between them, Paul didn't care.

"You're right. And...and I was wrong. About how I looked at you. About... other things to, and I'm just trying to...to fix things," Paul said, causing her to once again shake her head "no."

"I've got work to do," she said, as she started to walk away.

"You ran away from home, right?" Paul said. Linda stopped, nervously eyeing some nearby police officers, before returning closer to his table.

"What the hell are you doing, Paul?"

"I...I just want to help."

"Yeah well, you can help by fucking off."

"Just give me five more minutes, and if you don't like what I have to say, then that's exactly what I'll do, Linda."

He placed a hundred-dollar bill on the table, so that she could see it.

"What's that? You think I want you to pay me to fuck you?" she asked, struggling to hold back tears, "You know...I've been waiting tables for the last six months trying not to do that shit anymore."

"No, it's money for you to get out of here. To go back home."

"I'm not looking for charity, or for you to fix me," she said, sobbing. The tears started to stream down her face, just as another customer called out for a refill. "Just a minute!"

"It's not charity. It's just one friend helping out another, and it's not you that I'm trying to fix," Paul said, as he got up from the table, leaving the hundred there, and getting close to her. "Look, you do what you want with the money, but if there's ever been a time where you thought about getting out of here, I'm begging you...use it to do just that."

He leaned in and kissed her gently on the forehead. "Goodbye, Linda."

She watched Paul walk out, before slowly picking up the money off the table. She quickly wiped away the tears, before heading over to the other customer for their requested refill, carrying on with business as usual.

━━━━

Paul slowly opened the office door to his editor's office, to find Mr. Mackey sitting at his desk, and...holding a shotgun that was strategically pointed directly at him.

"Come in. Have a seat," he said, as Paul moved inside the space, his eyes glued to the shotgun, as he carefully sat.

"Now...slowly take out your gun, and put it on the desk," Mr. Mackey continued, causing Paul to look at him, obviously surprised at his insight. "Don't insult my intelligence. I know you're carrying."

Paul slowly reached into his waistband, pulled out his gun, and placed it on the desk.

"Now, is our little problem solved, Paul?"

"I need to know my family is safe," Paul replied, causing Mr. Mackey to clear his throat, before nodding his head toward the aimed shotgun.

"Not sure you're in any position to dictate terms."

"Then I'm walking out of here, and you can shoot me in the back."

"Either way I'd be getting what's in that satchel, so why get yourself killed?"

Paul stood up, his eyes dark with fury and vengeance. "Because you threatened my wife!"

"That was business. Now sit down!" Mr. Mackey fired back, but Paul didn't sit. Instead, he moved to the side of the desk, removing it as an obstacle between the two of them and prompting Mr. Mackey to pivot in order to keep the gun trained on him. "Sit the fuck down!"

Paul held up the leather satchel. "If you want this, then you're going to need to tell me that my family is safe!" he said, holding it up and ensuring that Mr. Mackey got a good look at it.

"Give me the money!" Mr. Mackey screamed, his finger finding the trigger of the gun, just itching to pull it.

"Tell me they're safe!" Paul screamed back, as he started to move forward.

"Give me the fucking money, and yes...your family will be safe!" Mr. Mackey replied.

Paul stopped his forward movement, but he was now only a few inches away from the barrel of the shotgun.

"Thank you," Paul said, as he placed the leather satchel on the desk. Mr. Mackey opened it up, while still keeping the gun aimed at Paul, but neither action mattered much at this point, though, because as soon as Mr. Mackey peered inside the bag, Paul put his years of combat training to good use.

Paul lunged forward with his left arm, his open palm hitting the bottom of the shotgun, and knocking it upwards, causing Mr. Mackey to pull the trigger. The shot ended up harmlessly hitting the ceiling. Then Paul's right arm reached toward the back of the gun that was still pointed upward, grabbing it and swiftly disarming Mr. Mackey in the process. The whole event happened in mere seconds, and marked the beginning of the end for Mr. Mackey. Paul smashed Mr. Mackey in the face with the shotgun, before dropping it on the floor and moving in for the kill with the hoodlum's knife in his hand.

Accompanied by an animalistic, guttural scream, the lightning-fast Paul plunged the knife into Mr. Mackey's subclavian artery in the front of his shoulder, before pulling it out just as quickly, only to stab the axillary artery under the armpit next, followed by slicing the knife across the internal/external jugular vein on the side of his neck. Then he was on to the common/internal iliac artery under the intestines, before the blade tore through the femoral veins in the front of the thigh, and finally ended by the knife being stabbed into the subclavian vein/artery behind Mr. Mackey's collarbone.

Mr. Mackey tried to speak, but all he could manage were a series of horrendous gurgling sounds throughout the process. It was overkill 101, and it left Paul completely covered in Mr. Mackey's blood, as the lifeless body fell to the floor with a thud.

I finally had some answers.

Paul stood over him, panting like a winded animal, before slowly moving to sit behind the desk.

And I finally had my ending.

Smiling from ear to ear, he took out his notebook, and started to write as the contents of the leather satchel were finally revealed. It was empty.

Meanwhile, in the lounge area of the upscale New York apartment, the doorman handed Chevy a handwritten note from Paul, that read: A token of respect, but now I'm out. –Paul

What happens as the cracks start to grow, from tiny spiderwebs...

The doorman placed a large trash bag on the bar in front of Chevy, who opened it to reveal it was filled with cash.

*...to something just short of full-blown chasms, that are as far and
as wide as the human eye could ever see?*

Back in the editor's office, Paul paused his writing, looking down to see Mr. Mackey's body had continued to bleed out with the massive quantity of blood starting to pool on the floor.

*You fill those cracks with the blood of the wicked, and in doing so,
you keep the foaming animals with their jaws open, and their teeth
bared to the world, at bay. That way, hopefully we won't have to
actually scratch that innate and primal itch, or...*

Mr. Mackey's blood started to find its way into the various cracks and crevices.

*...or break completely again like we did last night. The righteous
shall rejoice when he seeth the vengeance; He shall wash his feet in
the blood of the wicked. –Psalms 58:10*

Paul finished writing the last few lines, then got up with his notebook in hand before his boots walked through the spilled blood on their way out the door.

Still covered in blood, Paul walked into his tiny New York apartment, and made a beeline for the fridge for a cold one. He opened it up, quickly downed the brew, and opened another, as he proudly stared at his blood-covered notebook on the counter. Paul finished the second beer just as quickly as the first and was about to open a third, but stopped when he heard a baby crying in the other room.

"What the –?" he said to himself, as he put the beer down and slowly made his way into the bedroom.

The crying continued, as Paul slowly made his way over to the crib to find his daughter, awake and fussy.

"Hey, hey...it's okay. Shhhh. Shhhh," he said gently, as he picked her up and held her close, comforting her.

Slowly the baby started to calm down.

"Paul?" Valentina called out.

"What are you guys doing home?"

The bundle of blankets in the bed started to stir. "I was worried about you with the blackout, so we took a cab home a few hours ago," she replied, as she turned around to see the sheer horror of her blood-covered husband, holding their innocent baby. "Oh my God...Paul?" she gasped, as she quickly got up from bed, eyes-wide, and raced over to him. "Are you okay?"

"I've...I've never been better," Paul replied, and he clearly meant it.

"What happened?" she asked, her eyes still filled with worry and fear.

"I finally finished my book, and...and I really think this is going to be the one," he said, smiling from ear to ear, still holding the baby, and still very much covered in blood.

Needless to say, it was quite the sight, and quite the end to his story.

THE END

About the Author

This is Michael's first novel, adapted from one of his screenplays, and writing it has been a lifelong dream.

Born and raised in Massachusetts and the oldest of two boys raised primarily by their mother, Michael studied business at Boston College, before moving to California to pursue screenwriting and directing, where he has written and directed such films as NO TEARS IN HELL, a feature film based on the true story of the Siberian Ripper, along with HUNTER'S MOON, which he also produced. The film stars Thomas Jane, Jay Mohr, and Sean Patrick Flanery, and was released by Grindstone and Lionsgate.

Michael also wrote THE DEVIL'S TRAP, starring Bruce Dern, and co-wrote HANGMAN, starring Al Pacino, Karl Urban, and Brittany Snow. In 2020, he wrote the Mexican film, SIN ORIGEN for famed horror director, Rigoberto Castaneda. Most recently he was the co-writer for the soon-to-be-released action film THE ISLAND, starring Michael Jai White.

In the television space, he spent time in Armenia, where he wrote and co-directed the 16-episode series PURGATORY for Popstar TV. Previously he did a polish on all ten episodes of the show NOVA VITA, starring Dean Norris and Titus Welliver, along with being the show's supervising producer and co-directing the series.

Michael loves what he does, but he loves even more knowing that no matter what he creates, ultimately his lasting legacy will be his three children—Gavin, Joaquin, and Lily—who are without a doubt his world.